*The*
# Hidden People

collected stories

Joe McGowan

*To Bridget and Fergus, Rían and Matilda, Cormac, Síofra and Róisín:*
*'the book of my numberless dreams.'*

No part of this publication may be reproduced or transmitted
in any form or by any means, electronic or mechanical,
including photocopying, recording or any information or
retrieval system, without the prior permission of the author,
Joe McGowan, in writing.

First published in 2014 by: Aeolus Publications
The author wishes to acknowledge and thank all those
writers whose verse or prose is included in this book.

© Joe Mc Gowan / www.sligoheritage.com
Email: joemcgowan@sligoheritage.com
ISBN 978-0-9521334-6-9

Design and Typesetting, Martin Corr
Typeset in Livory 10pt and 17pt
Printed on 80gsm Valletta Wove
Printed by Gutenberg Press Limited

*'Let us go forth, the tellers of tales, and seize whatever prey the heart longs for, and have no fear. Everything exists, everything is true, and the earth is only a little dust under our feet.'*
(W.B. Yeats, *The Celtic Twilight*)

# *The* Hidden People

collected stories

# CONTENTS

| | | |
|---|---|---|
| 1. | COLD WAR IN KILLAWADDY | 11 |
| 2. | VIETNAM | 32 |
| 3. | COSMOS | 70 |
| 4. | THE BITTER SEASONS | 84 |
| 5. | THE HIDDEN PEOPLE | 132 |
| 6. | THE MATCHMAKER AND THE PILL | 140 |
| 7. | LAND OF THE FREE | 182 |
| 8. | THE STOLEN CHILD | 206 |
| 9. | WHERE THE GOOD MEN IS | 221 |

# 1

## COLD WAR IN KILLAWADDY

In the village of Killawaddy lived three Important People: Jeremiah Dillon the postmaster, Mrs. O'Callaghan-Guckian the hotelkeeper, and Fr. Moriarty the Catholic Curate. Being small farmers and fishermen — plus one modest shopkeeper — the rest of the inhabitants, the Lesser People, didn't matter very much. Except of course to themselves. There was no wall or visible line to separate the classes but it was there just the same. Quite possibly the distinction wasn't much noticed at the time, but with hindsight all is clear.

The Important People may indeed have been cognisant of their greater importance than the Lesser People but it being a small village, didn't rub their noses in it. After all their very existence depended on the operation of a kind of symbiosis between the classes. It was a fragile balance. There was an inclination for the Important People or IPs to flaunt their superiority but the peasantry were a volatile lot and such exhibitionism might upset the delicate balance of village life, or worse still, invite ridicule. The Lesser People or LPs had a razor-sharp wit and were good at cutting people down to size, particularly those who had an exaggerated sense of their greatness. The Lesser People knew their place but while they were quite happy to find it themselves, God help the Important Person who would try to put them in it!

There was social division too among the LPs but that doesn't concern us much. Suffice it to say that persons who burned turf considered themselves superior to those that burned 'sticks' or firewood. The turf burners were hard working people who spent most of their summer on the bog cutting and saving turf or in the meadows saving hay. The stick burners, like the fabled grasshopper, whiled away the summer in pleasant pursuits. When winter arrived, having no turf to burn, they had to go to the woods for fuel. This social distinction was also clearly signalled by which chimney wafted the pungent wood smoke on dark winter nights and which smelled of the fragrant turf. Additionally the wood burners, liking their beds more than spade or shovel, didn't generally 'put up smoke' till about midday. It was a sure giveaway as there was no other way to boil the breakfast kettle.

The LPs, having little, were happy enough with their lot. After all it was their inheritance, and life remained little changed from one generation to the next. They never aspired to owning a hotel, a Post Office or a Presbytery. This was the '60s and although times were beginning to change they might as well wish for the moon. If they had the turf home and dry, the hay saved by the end of the year and a good harvest, they were happy and contented. What more out of life would a person want! To want more was to become discontented, as more wasn't on offer. Unless of course you emigrated. When that happened the waters of community life closed in around the vacuum and pretty soon you didn't matter anymore, one way or another — to anyone.

The IPs were different. They expected more out of this life than it was giving them at any particular moment. Even within *their* small ranks thrived an uneasy rivalry. Being IPs they had a certain status to achieve and maintain, and each one felt they were the one predominant in their particular social order. Having different professions it wasn't always easy to tell who was top dog. A bit like comparing apples to oranges to bananas.

Mrs O'Callaghan-Guckian — no one ever knew her first name, as her stern countenance forbade any such familiarities — was a small stout woman of formidable bearing that made up for her lack of stature. Her gift, perfect for her calling was, chameleon like, the ability to change her accent to the accent of whatever particular tourist she was talking to: if it was an American then she had an American accent; if English then it was an English accent, and so on. The locals didn't like this one little bit. They liked people to be themselves. Being unaffected in their own lives they derided this posturing in others, just as much as they did the emigrant who returned after a short while abroad sporting a foreign accent: American or English.

The Postmaster, a man of diminutive stature with a corkscrew face in which were set two shifty little eyes, had a self important air about him unbefitting the modest establishment of which he was master. His pate was crowned with a few tired strands of grey hair that, although arranged carefully and brilliantined in place, stood perpetually on end and were of absolutely no help in camouflaging its shining nakedness.

Jeremiah was postmaster, grocer and commandant in charge of the one telephone line in and out of the village. No one else in the community was deemed competent enough to use the device — and Jeremiah would have no truck with any spalpeen or brat who had the audacity to think that they could put their paws on it. Like a little black Buddha it sat inscrutably on a nicely polished brown mahogany table in the hallway: a mystical oracle, a sacred object to be approached with reverence and awe.

If a farmer had a sick cow and needed to ring a vet it was to the Post Office and Jeremiah they had to go. On occasions like this he took up a protective stance beside the exotic instrument, took instructions sourly, and with exaggerated flourishes vigorously wound the little handle— there was no dial — that sent alarms jangling on Miss Mulligan's switchboard in the main Post Office in the neighbouring village of Kilnamuck who in turn plugged cables in and out of a confusing array of receptacles that allowed Jeremiah's message to travel further along circuitous avenues that conveyed the word about the sick cow to the GPO in Sligo and from there to the vet.

No one could do it as good as Jeremiah.

It was, however, an unfair competition as no one else ever got the chance. Only he got to wind the little handle and speak importantly into the mouthpiece. Indeed there were some in the village who claimed they were forever traumatised by the experience and, on emigrating, required counselling before they could summon up the nerve to pick up the phone and make a call in their adopted land.

The calls were mainly for farm animals as by the time their health was assured there was not much left over for people. The cows, calves and farm stock were the small farmers life's blood. Without his animals a farmer and his family were reduced to destitution. Ringing the vet at all was a last resort. It was tried only after exhausting all the folk remedies: elfstones, garlic & soot, *poitín*, water from a holy well and so on.

It was often the case that by the time the vet got to the farmer he was met with a buzz of conversation from neighbours, faith healers and practitioners of herbal medicine gathered about the byre where lay the sick cow. The telephone system, acting almost as an open bush telegraph, left no secrets and by the time the vet got there it was common knowledge to everyone from Killawaddy to Sligo, a distance of twenty six miles, that such and such a farmer had a sick cow.

At a time when everyone 'kept a book' in the local shop, Jeremiah frowned on the practice. A sign he had printed and displayed in a prominent position at the counter often provoked comment and knowing smiles:

'In this world of doubt and sorrow,' it read, 'The most doubtful words are, I'll pay you tomorrow.'

The locals indulged all his little idiosyncrasies as having spent his early years in America strange behaviour was expected.

Killawaddy itself was a picture postcard seaside town of, as noted previously, farmers and fishermen, and the occasional tourist who, when he discovered its peace and tranquillity, kept the secret to himself. Being once a garrison town the place previously had an even higher order: the VIPs or Anglo-Irish 'gentry', as they were known, who during the summer months played and pursued their idle pleasures along the seafront. This seafront, on the Eastern side of the village, was wholly taken up with the buildings and appurtenances necessary to the enjoyment of great wealth: a kind of holiday village in which there was a harbour, golf course, stables, carriage houses and an expansive green lawn for the playing of croquet and cricket. In time, the LPs were removed from the Eastern side when the holiday village was established. This served to clear the way for redevelopment and ensured that the humble two and three roomed thatched cottages of the peasants were kept well out of sight.

In this pecking order the overlords disdained both the IPs and the LPs, or at best accepted them with condescending toleration, as after all, being long subjugated, they were an inferior lot at all levels of their curious, inbred social interactions. The collaborators and 'crowbar brigades', having no allegiance to flag or country, were tolerated as being essential to control the rebellious and tear down their neighbours houses when evictions were necessary. There was of course also the, 'hewers of wood and drawers of water' whom it was necessary to put up with being needed for domestic chores such as cooking and cleaning!

Occasionally the VIPs rode their carriages along *Ros na Rí*, that windswept western side to view the source of their wealth: the 'peasantry', they who worked hard on their smallholdings and, mostly, paid their rents on time. In return they were allowed to live, work and farm on their small squares of reasonably arable land; land that was allotted to their forbears long ago by a dubious legal contrivance known as 'surrender and re-grant'. This was a ruse by which the Irish chieftains were compelled to surrender their land to the Crown upon which it was re-granted to them. The snag was, of course, that it no longer legally belonged to them and was, in any case, confiscated eventually and given to Cromwellian settlers.

The disgruntled peasantry, being an unsettled lot, were entirely ungrateful for all this 'benevolence' of their masters. Smouldering resentment led eventually to rebellion, one of many, that finally swept away the old order. The VIPs with their English accents and English ways disappeared and were replaced by the IPs. Little was changed for the LPs except that they felt a freedom of the soul they had never felt before — and they didn't have to pay rents to foreigners. Where farm work was concerned their smallholdings still had to be painstakingly tilled and cultivated as before. Land was a hard and unrelenting taskmaster brought to fruitfulness only by the laborious wielding of crude but efficient hand tools: rake, fork, spade, shovel or horse-drawn plough.

The trouble with land though was that there was never enough of it! This scarcity, leaving few opportunities for expansion, was bound to lead to conflict from time to time.

And it did.

In addition to the Post Office Jeremiah had a holding of land on which he kept a few cows and bullocks. Fr. Moriarty had only a small plot on which to feed his one cow and often had to resort to the 'long acre', the grass margin alongside the road, to feed the animal. Both had their eye on a little house and plot of land owned by Malachai Clinton, an eccentric and elderly gentleman. Children went quietly to bed when threatened that Malachai would come and take them away in a bag if they didn't. Adults avoided meeting him when they could. Which, when you think about it, was no great disgrace as they also avoided meeting the priest if there was any way out of it. Priests in general were held more in fear than respect and you never knew what misdemeanours or delinquency in one's recent past they might have unearthed.

Grown men left the road and went out of their way across fields rather than meet or challenge the power of a priest. The threat of '*I'll put horns on you!*' was taken seriously. Few defied the man with the collar but there were some brave souls willing to risk eternal damnation or the embarrassment of horns on their forehead when put to it.

Fr. Moriarty's cow once broke away from him and seeing the Postmaster on the road ahead called out:

'Quick! Block that cow for me!'

'Bugger off, block her yourself, d'ye think I have nothing else to do!' Jeremiah shouted back. He was in a particularly bad mood that same day. It was hot, the warble fly was about, and he had cattle of his own breaking through fences. Even on a good day he didn't think it was right for a priest to be a farmer anyway, even if it was on such a small scale.

'If ye don't I'll stick ye to the road,' the priest shouted back at him.

'If you're that good, why don't you stick the cow to the road,' Jeremiah replied, not unreasonably, and he legged it off down the lane and out of sight as fast as shoe leather could carry him.

Malachai's land was adjacent to the Post Office and would serve nicely to enlarge Jeremiah's holding. Acquisition of the property would mean that Fr. Moriarty would no longer have to resort to the Long Acre. Both men visited the old man: one to administer to his material needs and the other to the spiritual.

Regarding religion, Malachai in that too was a man of uncertain habits: he either didn't go to Mass at all, condemning out of hand priest and pulpit, or went in an excess of remorse and enthusiasm for as long as those impulses lasted. When he did go his habits were a distraction to the regular Mass goers who either prayed their rosary or followed the Latin Mass quietly and devoutly. Following a long absence Fr Moriarty had convinced Malachai for the umpteenth time that his soul was surely going to hell if he didn't start to attend Mass regularly. Easter was coming up, it was a good time to make a fresh start, and he expected to see him there.

Easter was a special time for Killawaddy and indeed for Christians all over the world.

Christ's death was mourned on Good Friday and the Resurrection celebrated joyously on Easter Sunday. Even the sun danced on that eventful morning.

The ceremonies were crowned by a vigorous denunciation of Satan. Everyone was glad to do this as from birth they had been warned of Lucifer and his legions and how they travelled the earth with their evil intentions. Satan and his temptations were lurking everywhere: in dance halls, on country roads, even in their beds at night. No one wanted to meet *him* on the way home from rambling on dark nights — and, at the time this was not at all an unusual occurrence. Hadn't he frightened the life out of a young girl at a dancehall in Tooreen in Co. Mayo whom he attempted to lure away with him; and weren't there several instances of card players being challenged to a game on the way home from a night's card playing by a dark, mysterious stranger!  A stranger, whom many a lucky escapee discovered, just in the nick of time, had cloven feet.

No chance then of winning a game from him!

With Satan the stakes were high.  It was not money he was after but the player's immortal soul.

A pre-emptive strike was what was called for, and no time better than Easter to do it.  Better to let him know right from the start, to declare publicly and officially, that he was not welcome.

There was a stir as this highlight of the evening approached. Everyone lit his or her candles and the ceremony commenced.

'Do ye renounce Satan?'

There was an evangelistic fire in Fr. Moriarty's voice.

'We do.'

It wasn't good enough.  This would never do.  There wasn't enough sincerity in their voices.  He glared down at them.

'I can't hear ye!  Do ye renounce Satan?'

**'We do.'**

'I still can't hear ye!  Say it like ye mean it!

**Do ye renounce Satan**?

**'We renounce Satan!**

**'An'... and... fuck him as well!** an angry voice, loud and clear, erupted from the back of the chapel. Every head turned this way and that way like a field of nodding daffodils, to get a better view, and sure enough there was Mad Malachai on the kneeler behind the last seat carried away by the occasion and overflowing with zeal and passion.

The focus of attention immediately turned from Fr. Moriarty and Lucifer to Malachai. They were sure the priest cracked just the faintest smile; everyone else giggled and tittered quietly. The priest however maintained his decorum and announced sternly that if anyone in the congregation couldn't act with dignity and respect for the house of God they were welcome to leave — at once.

Neither the postmaster or the priest would admit it, possibly even to themselves, but it was obvious to everyone else that their visits were motivated by factors other than the welfare of the old man. Although never breaking into open hostility the two pillars of the community, when they met, exchanged baleful glares. Jeremiah saluted the priest (or more correctly the Host that the priest always carried), as was the custom of the time, and the priest acknowledged the courtesy with a frosty nod. It was the equivalent, on a small scale, of the Cold War that at that time was developing on the international stage between the Soviets and the Western world but, at least to the villagers of Killawaddy, it was no less important. As the poet once said: 'Gods make their own importance.' The question often kicked around the firesides at night was to which of the temptations the old man would succumb: Heaven in the form of a hot meal now and again in this life, or the promise of everlasting Life in the next.

Father Moriarty came from that mother lode of priests and nuns: Roscommon. A stern man of the old school he led his flock most of the time, but had no hesitation in driving them when he felt circumstances demanded it. He favoured the direct approach and there was no waltzing around delicate issues as he teased out God's laws and desires during his sermons:

> *'High in front advanced,*
> *The brandished sword of God before them blazed,*
> *Fierce as a comet.'*

His flock was left in no doubt as to what was right or wrong as he thundered his disapproval of the villagers indiscretions and failures and apprised them of the generous width of the path that led to Hell, the ease with which it could be travelled, and the narrowness of the righteous way that led to Heaven.

His sermons, when St. Patrick's Day came around, were intense. Delivered with fire and passion his homily on this national holiday was invariably about emblems. Ireland's symbol was the little shamrock, he explained, chosen long ago by Patrick to demonstrate to our pagan ancestors the mystery of three persons in one, the Divine Trinity. The leek, he told his audience, was the symbol of Wales, and the thistle the chosen insignia of Scotland. For England's badge he reserved special mention. Of all the nations of the earth, he proclaimed, his voice rising wrathfully, the red rose was England's symbol. And 'well red it might be', he declared, 'smeared as it is with the blood and gore of generations of Irish men and women.'

He paused in his sermons and cast dark glances when there was a particularly noisy barrage of coughing or foot shuffling during one of his dissertations. He let his annoyance at those who were perpetually late for Mass be known, and complained occasionally — but he could tolerate these little distractions.

If there was one thing that was completely unacceptable to him, and annoyed him above everything else it was the men's habit of huddling in the porch at the back of the church while the front seats remained empty. He tried everything. He wheedled; he cajoled; he threatened; he implored. Well aware of his disapproval, and not having any good reason to be at the back, they stared back at him with shifty eyes. But it was still no good. From such a safe distance, his entreaties fell on deaf ears. He even tried psychology. Centuries of subservience to foreigners and tyrannical landlords had bred an inferiority complex that still lingered within us even though those days were gone, he reasoned. Dressed and fed as good as the best of them we could now take our proud place at the front of any gathering.

Still no good.

On rare occasions some of the weaker souls shuffled sheepishly up the church to a seat, but the hard core remained in the rear, immovable and unbending.

It wasn't that they were defying the priest; it was just that they were comfortable there and felt that God's grace was just as abundant at the back of the church as at the front. It had the added advantage that you could come in late without being noticed and away like a flash after the last blessing. Sure, they knew it was a mortal sin to miss Mass on Sundays or Holydays of Obligation but where was it written that they had to be up at the front of the church? And what about the lesson of the Pharisee and the Publican? Didn't Christ himself say that the last would be first and the first last? Anyway, didn't everyone know them oul' craw-thumping hypocrites that was the first at the altar rails would steal the milk out of yer tay once they got outside?

*'The longer the rosary beads the bigger the hypocrite!'*

Once or twice, following the Biblical example of Christ and the moneychangers, Fr. Moriarty's temper flared and he charged the defiant back door mob like an avenging angel. Priestly garments flying he sped down the aisle in a surprise attack — but it was no good, they fled in every direction except up to the front seats. The porch was empty by the time he reached it. It was a stalemate, but he never gave up and the variety and unpredictability of his efforts at filling the front seats made trips to Mass that much more entertaining for many years.

Christmas was a time of year when, all squabbles forgotten, Fr. Moriarty was the undisputed leader of the community. Differences put aside for a while a quiet peace pervaded the village.

'A happy Christmas to ye,' everyone said as they made their way to Mass on Christmas morning.

Entering the church, the crib across from the confession box was a hushed island of peace in the moving throng. The Christ child in a bed of straw stretched out welcoming arms. Plaster statues of Joseph and Mary, the shepherds, the farm animals, all were bathed in a warm light. It was the simplest and most touching thing the community would ever see at Christmas, or indeed any other time of the year. The two thousand year old message, a message of peace in a troubled world, was as relevant then as when the Christ child was born. Humbled before the Eternal message Important People as well as Lesser People knelt and prayed to the baby son of God the nuns had placed in the manger. When they were finished praying, a few straws from Christ's bed were teased out to hang up in the cow byre for good luck and prevention of disease. Other wisps were put behind the picture of the Sacred Heart in the kitchen as a blessing on the family.

A quiet peace pervaded the little chapel. The perpetual light of the red sanctuary lamp flickered and danced in front of the altar. Eternity dwelt here. As it was, is now, and ever shall be, world without end. Cares would wait for another day. The whole of Killawaddy's year was encompassed in this place, at this time. Big or small, lesser or greater, what else mattered in the end except the salvation of their souls:

'*Gloria in excelsis Deo*' burst forth, swelled and echoed around the walls and roof of the little chapel as the choir, accompanied by the organ, sang out on this, one of the biggest occasions of their year.

The Joyful mysteries of the Rosary were recited — and as if

that wasn't enough, after that the Litany of Praises:

*'Holy Mother of God'*, the reciter droned.

*'Pray for us'*, everyone responded in unison.

*'Holy Virgin of virgins'*

*'Pray for us'* they chanted.

*'Spiritual Vessel'*, it went on, *'Mystical Rose, Tower of Ivory, House of Gold'*, until at last there was an air of resignation in everyone's voice:

*'Pray for us'*, they repeated wearily.

Nobody ever questioned how it was that any woman could be a Tower of Ivory or a House of Gold. It was just another one of those mysteries of Faith that were scattered plentifully throughout their religion. Still, with God anything was possible — and it was nice to conjure up images of ivory towers at Christmas. They seemed so exotic, and made a nice change from the weekday commonplace of turnip fields, warble flies, potato pits and cowdung!

Sanctuary bells pealed a jangle warning. The celebrant of the Mass, decked in white chasuble and flowing alb, swept to the altar preceded by a retinue of altar boys. Turning to the tabernacle, eyes raised to heaven, he commenced a practised rote:

*'Introibo ad altare Dei.'*

*'Ad Deum qui litificat juventutem meum.'*

*'Quia tu es, Deus, fortituda mea, quare me repulisti? Et quare tristis incedo dum affligit me inimicus?'*

It might have been a Druid chant.

The priest on the altar, intermediary between man and God,

robed arms outstretched, faced the altar as he intoned the Latin Mass. Behind him, his congregation, segregated as the etiquette of the time demanded, followed the Mass on their Missals. Women knelt on one side of the chapel with heads covered as a mark of respect to God in His house; obedient to some strange forgotten dictum, men knelt on the other side, their heads uncovered for the same reason: husbands on one side, wives on the other.

Only the Important People broke this code and worshipped on whichever side they chose. The community, noticing this strange behaviour, accepted the idiosyncrasies of the exalted classes with a smile and a knowing shake of the head. Why should the repositories of such wealth and self importance be restricted by the same rules that bound ordinary mortals, they mocked?

Father Moriarty was convinced that God got it right when he said it was easier for a camel to go through the eye of a needle than for a rich man to enter God's kingdom. Wealth as far as he was concerned, at least on a Sunday, was nothing but a hindrance.

The LPs took great comfort from this message and the promise of greater things to come in the afterlife. The point, as far as anyone could make out, was lost on the IPs.

'We must store our riches in heaven,' the priest insisted, 'where the Bible tells us that neither rust nor moth can consume.'

One way of paving the way to Paradise was to contribute in generous measure to the various church collections held throughout the year. Of these, the Christmas collection was the most important. The congregation, particularly the business people, were expected to give generously.

For years, a contribution of one pound was sufficient guarantee for the hotel owner, Mrs. O'Callaghan-Guckian, to head the list and secure a top position in this social order.

Mass goers thought her a perfect Christian. She confidently knelt when she was supposed to kneel, stood when it was time to stand, and sat when sitting was what was required. At the Consecration of the bread and wine the sanctuary bell rang six distinct times. At each ringing it was customary to alternately bow and straighten the head. Mrs. Guckian's head was always in the raised position at the last bell. Always. Which when you think about it seems where it should be. This may seem a small matter and hardly an article of faith but not everyone got it right. Depending on whether you bowed or remained upright at the first bell determined where your head would be at the last ring. For most their head could be up or down. But Mrs. G always got it right. For those uncertain about such protocols they too could always attain perfection by watching her out of the corner of their eye.

A pound was a lot of money then, enough to buy groceries for one week for an average size family. Some gave what they could afford, other contributions varied in size according to the importance, real or imagined, or the social aspirations of the donor.

Further down the list, the majority of offerings were from the workers and farmers, who usually weighed in with anything from an unpretentious one shilling and sixpence to two shillings.

Contributors were noted and placed on a list according to the size of their donation, the largest, of course, being first. The list was read out on the Sunday after Christmas. Attention peaked as the congregation listened intently to find out if Mrs. O'Callaghan-Guckian had held on to the top position or if, maybe the Postmaster, Jeremiah Dillon, or some other aspirant had displaced last year's winner.

Yes, the collection was sure to be a talking point when Mass was over and the residents of Killawaddy gathered outside the chapel gates for the weekly chat and exchange of the week's news. When the moment of truth arrived the congregation shuffled, eased into a comfortable position, shuffled some more, coughed noisily and fell into an expectant silence. The priest turned around with his list and the show started.

'Mrs. O'Callaghan-Guckian, one pound,' he commenced.

Well, no surprises there. Mrs. O'Callaghan-Guckian, who always arrived late as befitted important people, and always sat in the front row, a fox fur draped around her neck in the fashion of the time, straightened herself importantly the tall feather in her hat fluttering triumphantly as, once again, she found herself in the winner's enclosure. Her fox fur was a wonder to anyone who saw it and you could only feel sorry for the poor thing as it hung there around her neck, its little beady unseeing eyes and limp paws dangling helplessly over the undulating curvature of a vast bosom that would nearly graze a cow.

The list went on and everyone lost interest as the priest reached the one and sixpences. But where was Jeremiah Dillon, they wondered idly? His name hadn't featured in its usual place, generally well above the ten-shilling mark, as befitted his status in the community.

Then suddenly it came.

'Jeremiah Dillon, one shilling,' the priest read.

An audible intake of breath rippled through the congregation as they were shocked into alertness again by the Postmaster's diminished position on the list.

Father Moriarty read the name once and then pausing for effect:

*'Jere — miah —Dillon — one — shilling,'* he repeated again, spacing and emphasising the words, his voice shaking with indignation as it rose by several decibels.

A rustle of disbelief ran through the audience. What moment of misguided misanthropic folly had allowed Jeremiah to disturb the social equilibrium of the village? And at Christmastime too! What could it be?

Everyone knew of the rivalry between the two men.

Was the rumour true then that Malachai had finally signed over his property to Fr. Moriarty? And Jeremiah was now cash starved on account of putting his shillings aside to buy a bit of land on the open market. Or could it be that in a fit of pique, and vicious as a wasp, Jeremiah had decided to retaliate by curtailing his contribution to the priests welfare and, at the same time express his disapproval, in a very public way, of what he saw as the priest's unseemly greed? A move that had rebounded on him in no uncertain way.

This verbal battle of wills, fought in full public view, was the focal point of conversation in the village for weeks and everyone laughed as they repeated and savoured the priest's emphasis.

'Did ye hear him:

*"Jeremiah Dillon, one — shilling!*

***Jeremiah — Dillon — one — shilling!"***

They laughed as they mimicked the derision in the priest's voice and how he had cleverly and so subtly turned the tables. Jeremiah was a very pompous man and it was no harm to take him down a peg or two, everyone agreed. Father Moriarty hadn't scolded or spoken a single word of reprimand but, nevertheless, in a masterstroke of satirical emphasis, had come out of this one a clear winner. Marc Antony couldn't have done it better. Brutus was defeated and a lesson taught to anyone who dared think they could cross the priest in a public manner and get away with it.

After that Jeremiah always kept a respectable place on the Christmas list and in the community, but like the March blizzard of '47 or the Night of the Big Wind, the 'Christmas of the Gladiators' was etched forever in the memories of the citizens of Killawaddy.

# 2

## VIETNAM

The thunder of surf breaking on the *Ros na Rí* cliffs at Killawaddy filtered into Conor's consciousness. Must be a groundswell running he surmised sleepily. Pulling the blankets tightly around him he stirred uneasily with the prospect of bad weather. These crashing mountains of water shouted a warning of low pressure way out in the North Atlantic, weather systems that would soon bring gales and driving rain. Born to the clamour of the sea and aware of its changing moods he was accustomed to the sound — but this morning in his uneasy dreams he sensed something strangely different.

Gradually, in that state between sleeping and waking, when our nightmares become real or, gratefully, shadows in a dream, the awful realisation dawned on him that he was far, far from home. This was no familiar sound of seas, gentle or fierce, breaking on his *Ros na Rí* shore but the thunder of jet engines warming up at Maguire Air Force Base. Raising his head he perceived in the bleary dawn that the bed he was lying on was the upper tier of an unfamiliar steel bunk. A thin cold light sifted into the room. With it came a sickening dread that clawed at his stomach. Shapes, blurry in the half-light, slowly came into focus revealing dozens of sleeping figures on similar metal bunks. He was not at home in Kilawaddy but in an army barracks in Fort Dix, New Jersey, USA. Hardly had he time to absorb the awfulness of it when the door burst open, the lights hammered on, and a burly black sergeant came charging, shouting into the room:

'Alright ladies, time to get up. Get the fuck up! How many times do I have to say it? What do you think this is? A fucking holiday camp. Move it! Move it! Move it! You motherfuckers, move it, your ass is grass today my beauties and I'm the lawnmower!'

ॐ

Just a few weeks before, and barely six months after his arrival in the USA, Conor received his draft notice to report for an 'Armed Forces Physical Examination'. Devastated by the summons his first instinct was flight! How could he give up two years of his life to a country that was not his, and to which he owed nothing?

Since his arrival in the 'Promised Land' he had made a good start, worked hard, sent money home and was apprenticed as a carpenter. Was it all to be for nothing now? To where could he run? He was a stranger in a foreign country. He had no friends apart from the relatives who had sponsored his immigration. He should be grateful, they said. It was an honour to serve in the Armed Forces of his adopted land. He was in America now and owed a debt of gratitude to the U.S.A.

This advice seemed somewhat incongruous to him, as the youth of America, including his cousins, didn't seem at all anxious to be drafted and avoided it by every means possible: college, conscientious objector, disability, feigned or real.

His short taste of freedom and opportunity was at an end. Yearning to break free from the servitude of farm life at home was he now going to be brought into a new servitude? He had promised his parents he would go away for a few years, earn some money and return with a nest egg from the Land of Plenty. It would change their lives, bring them everything they dreamed of but could never have. However he couldn't go home now; it was too soon; he had no nest egg — and there was nothing to which he could return in Kilawaddy. Of work there was plenty, of financial reward: none. How could he go back now and risk being the butt of ridicule as someone who had returned a failure even before he started?

It was unthinkable.

ૡ

At the beginning of each new year the cycle started all over again. It was a treadmill that his father had trod in his time and his father before him, and his father again before that, for as long back as anyone could remember — and beyond.

Conor wanting more than a bleak hand to mouth existence announced his decision to leave. His shocked parents tried to hold him. They pleaded and offered every inducement they could think of, but it was no good. There must be a better life elsewhere and it would be only for a few years he assured them. He would come back when he had a nest egg saved.

Peter Mc Morrow, Conor's father, a sinewy armed man in his sixties, lived for his family and small farm and squeezed the most he could out of every square foot. He would not be conscious of it but his was the custodianship of this darkened earth, his inheritance that of the many generations before him; they that had drawn their sustenance from it, nurtured and cared for it. This land was not just a commodity, it was the very essence of their being, it had made their bones and flesh.

Short in stature but wiry as an eel he viewed the world evenly from two earnest brown eyes set in a wind and weather-beaten face. Bald as an egg with just a fringe around the sides he attributed the condition to lack of even the most basic sanitary facilities when he was interned in the Curragh during the Civil War. As there were no barbers in the Irish countryside it fell to Conor to cut his hair who was as grateful for its sparsity as his father was embarrassed. The old man's work driven ethic, oft repeated to Conor, was to 'never put off 'til tomorrow what you can do today'. 'Anything that's worth doin'at all is worth doin' right' was his mantra as he led by example, moulding perfect cocks of hay and handsome turf clamps or elegant stooks of rye and oats. He epitomised the bold peasantry of Goldsmith's village that 'once destroyed can never be supplied'.

Conor was taller than his father, just short of six feet, with smiling eyes topped by a mop of fair curly hair. A shy, earnest young fellow he made friends easily with his good nature and quiet ways. A sickly child when he was an infant his father was proud of the fine strong young man he had turned into.

It was a small village and every departing emigrant a big loss. They sympathised with Peter Mc Morrow's dilemma and chipped in with anxious advice:

'Conor, you have a good life here, what loss is on you,' Francie their next door neighbour advised. 'I can tell you for a fact that when the day comes the farm is yours. There's no one else will get it!'

'Good life! What's good about it Francie! You might be satisfied to work all year long, year after year, for nothing, nothing at all. What are you only a slave! There has to be something better.'

Ah Conor, d'ye know what you're talking about? Work for nothing! Look around you. Ye're as well off, or maybe better, than anyone else around here. Ye sell off the calves in the harvest time, your mother has a clutch of turkeys for the Christmas market, the hens for eggs for the table and more to pay for groceries, milk for the creamery, ye grow everything ye need, ye have your own potatoes, rye and oats: the grain for feed and the straw for thatching...'

'Better off than anyone else! But Francie, what's that only tuppence ha'penny looking better than tuppence! Don't you want to improve, add that porch to the kitchen that you always wanted and never have the money for. Have a holiday away from here. How many times have you come home from the fair with the same cattle you drove there in the morning and no sale nor money to pay the bills. Look at the parcels of clothes that come from America at Christmas. It must be a rich country. If I went there for a while I'd be sure to get work and make a lot of money and wouldn't I be able to send some home to help out!'

Conor's father was listening intently to the conversation and:

'Francie is right, he chipped in, 'the cow in the next field always has the longest horns, Conor. America is a fast country and doesn't suit everyone. My father handed on this farm to me, and his father before him to my father. The Mc Morrows have been on this land longer than anyone can remember. No one can remember them not being here. My brother Brian, like you, wanted more so he went to America. But he found no fortune, only the great depression of 1929 where he lost whatever small savings he had. When he left here he too intended to come back, but it went from year to year and it was always next year when he'd have enough to come home. The letters got fewer and fewer. He never did come back and we don't know where he is or what happened to him, whether he's dead or alive. Your mother and I are getting old, we have no one else and why would you want to leave us here alone? It would break your mother's heart!'

ॐ

Since his arrival at the army base yesterday all was confusion. A confrontation with a bad-tempered soldier bearing the yellow stripes of authority on his sleeve immediately set the tone. Mean as an enraged cobra he screamed abuse at all around him. Making short runs at anyone in his way he roared spittle-punctuated curses in their faces. He was black. Conor stared. He had never seen a black man at home. His only acquaintance with coloured people came from headlines in the Irish Press at home about race riots in far away Little Rock, Arkansas, and he was sympathetic. Now here was one of them in the flesh. With mad, hate-filled eyes he hurled Conor's duffle bag at him knocking him sideways. The frenzied corporal — the nametag on his uniform said he was Jackson — bellowed directions and abuse. No one, not even the meanest, dare answer back. They were trapped now in the maw of a mighty machine, their fate sealed when they raised their right hands at the induction centre to swear an oath ( some proudly, some reluctantly depending on whether they volunteered or were drafted) that bound them to, 'obey the orders of the President of the United States and the orders of the officers appointed over me.' This madman was only a small but vicious part of a complex whole.

The rules of normal society did not apply here. Bullying and bad manners were virtues inside the foreboding gates of Ft. Dix; it might well be a prison with its heavily guarded entrance, its fortified perimeter wall and rectangulated wooden barracks surrounding a central square. Hundreds of new recruits, all disoriented, were shunted here and shuttled there by ill mannered, abusive men in uniform, all with the bright yellow stripes of Authority; authority that had to be unquestioningly obeyed. No point in making matters worse. Yes Sergeant! No Sergeant! Get in line here to get a mattress, there to get sheets and blankets, another line to get uniforms, still another to pick up a wooden chest called a footlocker, all the time bullied and harassed and feeling stupid for not getting everything done better and quicker.

'Move, move, move, you worthless piece of shit.'

The following days passed in a haze of indoctrination, instruction, dehumanisation, robotizing. Locks, whether straight or curly, long or short, were shaven to the skin in a thirty-second sheep-shearing exercise. Everyone was issued identical footlockers and a clothes locker in which army regulations dictated the very order in which the various items of clothing, both civilian and military were to be placed. This was strictly enforced and woe betide the recruit who was caught out on inspection having his shorts where his shirts should be, his comb where the soap should be or the left sleeve of his shirt facing out if the right was mandated. It was not enough to make a tidy bed; it had to be made in a uniform fashion with regulation forty-five degree 'hospital corners'.

Before he left home and was plunged so unwillingly into this military life Conor pondered his parents future with anxiety. His father would not be able to carry on as well without his help and he was gradually having to take on more and more of the farm work. Seeming older than his sixty two years, he could see the old man was going down. He never complained but Conor could see that when he walked out to his work in the fields now he rested on the sod ditch more often, became breathless with very little exertion. His years on the run, often cold, wet and hungry in long nights spent on the hillside during Ireland's War of Independence, a hunger strike during the Civil War, those desperate years he never spoke about: all these now affected his health.

But the country of the old is a different place, a place populated by people — his father chief among them — with very different priorities to those of the young. While he observed its individuals their life was governed by concerns that were poles apart from anything with which Conor could empathise or understand. The country of the young was a different place too, and so it must be, theirs it is to build a new world and not be bound by the old.

Years of strict discipline bound him to obedience. So he worked on, suppressing his own desires and growing every day more discontented. The old longing would not leave. The futility of his existence, its endless toil with no reward daily troubled him. The weeks and months went slowly, laboriously by. Young people, schoolmates once, were emigrating from the village every day. He was past his twentieth birthday; life was passing him by. The weeks, the months, the seasons passed, and nothing was ever going to change. But it must. He must *make* it change. He was drowning in a life he didn't want, that he didn't choose. Smothered in his parents desires he was pulled one way, then another: he was selfish if he left, doomed to a life of mediocrity if he stayed. There were no other choices, no middle ground, no jobs, no opportunities in Ireland. It was the farm or emigration.

Spring turned to summer and summer to autumn. Conor worked with his father transforming waving fields of rye to stubble and neatly tied sheaves. A mellow harvest light goldened the hillside where they laboured. In the valley below and consecrated by the sun, stone bordered patchworks of yellow cornfields, green mown meadows dotted with cocks of hay and flowered potato fields sloped away to great vistas of mountain and sea. Out beyond Inishmurray and Carraigmore islands, on the horizon where sea met sky, mysterious and distant, lay the rims of the unknown world. 'Here be dragons' the ancient mapmakers wrote and one day soon it would be where Conor would find his.

Beauty is more easily appreciated with a full pocket and an easy mind; Conor saw here not beauty but only fetters of unending work and toil. Fistful by fistful he and his father cut the golden corn, securing the sheaves with a straw-made strap: grasp, shear, clean, tidy, tie. The stroke of the serrated blade on the straw made a rhythmic almost musical rasping: grasp, shear, clean, tidy, tie, seamlessly all day long. In the evening, like straw soldiers set against the skyline, the sheaves were built into tall stooks to dry.

Out in the bay, when fish were shoaling, the old man would sometimes pause in his labour, painfully straighten his back, and with an expert eye point out the great 'workings' of gulls moving across the sea that indicated the movement of the mackerel shoals through the bay. 'Workings' was the vernacular for the clouds of seagulls that dipped and wheeled in spiralling, white, raucous clouds on the shoals of silver sprat. He knew that, just as the gulls fed on the sprat from the air, so too the mackerel and other fish fed on them from underneath in the green depths of the ocean. 'Looks like *Pollachurry* is where the mackerel'll be in tonight,' he might say as he studied their movements and read the signs, or ' We'll head for *Leac Cam* this evening when the cows is milked, there's rain on the way, it'll be a fine soft evening and there could be a good take!'

Casting their lines off the rocky outcrops he went often with his father and the old experienced fishermen to try their luck. He even came to love it: the soft smell of rain on the way, the excitement when the shoals were in, the danger when there was a swell rising, the sea's breath on his face, whispering seductively in his ears.

On a memorable afternoon Catherine, his mother, had brought a soda cake, homemade butter and a stocking-wrapped bottle of tea to the field. A stout, jolly woman with a ready smile and plump cheeks, she was the foundation the family was built on. Her kitchen catered not only to the family's needs but to the needs of the farm animals as well. Here the cast iron pot was always on the boil with food for her flocks of hens, ducks and turkeys, cows and calves. In her spare time, of which she had none, she rushed to the meadow fields to fork, gather and build hay alongside her man when rain threatened.

'Ye're flying through it' she said proudly eying the day's work. 'You'll soon be hunting the hare over to Doyle's.' This was a reference to the belief that the spirit hare was chased from cornfield to cornfield bringing bad luck with it. In addition to losing status in the community the last reaper would have to feed the phantom hare for the winter months

All three now sat relaxed in the afternoon sunshine, a welcome respite from the morning's backbreaking toil. It didn't have to be backbreaking. A scythe would have been quicker and easier. Reaping hooks were hard going but they kept the straw tidy for thatching in a way the scythe could not. It's the way it was always done. Grain laden sheaves spread all around and well satisfied with his morning's work Peter sat listening to his wife's gossip: Annie Kelly was saying there was good prices for yearling heifers at Grange fair; Mary Murphy and her man got engaged; there was going to be a dance out in Clancy's tomorrow night to raise money for a poor family; Thomas Wymbs would be there with his accordion and Jimmy Warnock up from Tullnagreine — and wasn't Jimmy a gas man...

Conor could not take his inner tumult any longer, the worm eating away at his soul. His parents had a tight grip on him, if not physically then psychologically. There was no good time to re-introduce his unwelcome desires, the disclosure that would change their world. It's not that he had any deep understanding of the effect it would have on the continuity of their way of life so much as how he disliked unpleasantness. It was time to break free!

A deep breath and:

'Mam! Dad! Our cousins in America said they'd sponsor me out and send the fare if I wanted to go. I think I will.'

The chatter stopped. A sudden chill descended on the little field. A dark cloud had passed over their sun. Later he would remember the scene as in a photograph: the sunlit field, the sudden silence — and incongruously in that funereal stillness skylarks singing their hearts out in the joy of being. He remembered the dread feeling in the pit of his stomach, the skylarks, the crestfallen faces of his parents. In their small world all was changed in a shocking instant.

His mother stared disbelievingly. Fidgeting with a straw, she wound it round around her finger. His father spoke first:

'Conor if that's what you have to do then we can't stand in your way!' he said resignedly. 'But think long and hard before you go,' he said looking out across the bay. 'Take a look around you, take a good hard look. These fields, this place, will never be the same again. Remember this: once you go you can never come home again.'

A surge of relief flooded over Conor. It was a breakthrough! His heart leaped for joy. It was the consent, the approval he wanted and needed. Should he get up and jump and dance all around? He was going to be free, and that's all that mattered:

'Not at all Dad, sure why wouldn't I come back,' he said evenly containing the excitement within him. 'You'll see! I will come back and then it'll be a new beginning, a better time for us all!'

His father slowly shook his head and looking at his wife with a rueful smile:

'You can't put an old head on young shoulders,' he said.

Turning to Conor he elaborated,

'You'll see. You will change, the people you know will change, the fields will change, the world will move on, your world will turn to a new way of life and no passion of regret will bring it back. You mightn't see it now. You have a lot to learn and some day you will see the truth of what I'm telling you!'

❧

On arrival in Fort Dix Conor soon learned that it was the unwritten policy of the City Fathers of Draft Board No. 12 in Peekskill, New York to fill their quota with immigrants. Picking their cannon fodder from emigrant boats and later Boeing 707s they kept their own boys from suffering a similar fate. Land of the free and home of the brave indeed, he thought bitterly!

Assignment to companies was made on the basis of the first letter of an individual's surname  Last names beginning with

M. N or O were posted to Oscar Company, 4th Regiment. This meant that Conor, having the last name Mc Morrow, was soon surrounded by every Mc from Boston to Brooklyn — except for one oddity named Neas. This was quickly and good-humouredly addressed by christening him Mc Neas.

Indoctrination commenced immediately. A motley bunch of recruits was to be turned into soldiers in eight weeks. Rivalry with other Companies was encouraged. 'Second to none,' was the O Company motto. At all gatherings whether on parade or in the bleachers for lectures everyone stood to attention, like some herd of angry cattle, to bawl:

'Oscar 4th, second to none!'

'I can't fucking hear you. Shout it like you got a pair!'

'OSCAR FOURTH, SECOND TO NONE.'

'What are we?'

'We are the Ultimate Weapon!'

'Jesus H Fucking Christ, what a bunch of fucking pussies! I still can't fucking hear you!'

'WE ARE THE ULTIMATE WEAPON.'

'Get down and gimme ten.'

That meant ten push-ups. A penalty that was inflicted at random and for little or no reason. You didn't salute an officer properly?: ten push-ups in the dirt or maybe more. Your gig line wasn't straight (shirt buttons not in line with fly) ten push-ups, or more, depending on the sadistic tendencies of the NCO or officer.

Close order drill to a cadence made a platoon or company of men respond to set commands, to act as one: fall in; attention;

at ease; right shoulder arms; left shoulder arms; present arms; right face; left face; right dress; double time, forward march.

Tramp, tramp, tramp:

'Ain't no use in looking down/ There's no discharge on the ground/ Ain't no use in lookin back/ Your girlfriend's got your Cadillac/ I used to date a beauty queen/ Now I love my M14/ Standing tall and looking good/ We ought to be in Hollywood/ Ain't no use in going slow/ There's too many miles to go...'

Tramp, tramp, tramp.

' I left my gal away out west/ I thought this army life was best/ Now she's someone else's wife/ And I'll be marchin' the rest of my life/ Sound off: 1-2 Sound off: 3-4 Bring it on down: 1-2-3-4, 1-2, 3-4.'

Tramp, tramp, tramp.

'Idiotic stuff,' Conor thought — and what did all of this matter to him anyway?

෴

His thoughts often turned to what did matter to him and to the stressful days following his decision to leave. A sense of unreality pervaded the little household over the next days and weeks; a kind of twilight where the old certainties had vanished and only doubt remained. The anchor on which the Mc Morrow's had built their foundation had turned to shifting sand. Conor's course was irrevocably set, and so was that of his parents. He, voluntarily, to undertake a new voyage, his parents, reluctantly, to end theirs. Conor to go to a land about which he knew little, his parents to remain on the soil and sod they knew so well — thus exemplifying the optimism of youth and the resignation of age.

The fateful letter sent to the O'Connor aunts and cousins in Yorktown Heights, New York confirming that he would indeed accept their offer soon elicited his passage money. On the morning of Conor's departure the family was early on the move. Up and down their little stony road a pale morning sun was breathing light and warmth into the neat rows of thatched and whitewashed homes. From each chimney spirals of turf smoke ascended into calm; cocks announced the new day from their dunghills, hens complained, cattle bawled to be fed. In a babble of noise calves, ducks and cows greeted the new day in a chorus of noisy complaining. Just another normal day for everyone — except Conor

As in a wake a few neighbours were gathering in to sympathise the loss of a young man, not just to his family, but to the village as well. They spoke in whispers and low voices. Some, feigning sympathy, were secretly glad. Half happy the loss was not theirs they postured a solidarity they did not feel. A step down in social standing for one family they saw as a step up for theirs. The downfall of a family was not their loss. In this rivalry of the poor that simmered unspoken beneath the surface of village life, Catherine was always defiant: 'Have the name of it if ye never had it!' she would declare proudly in the teeth of hard times.

The 'American wake' was well named. Few would return; as in death most would never see their homes or family again. But there was always the hope they would come back. His mother, holding herself in check, busied herself making tea for the family and neighbours, fussed about Conor straightening his tie, brushed imaginary specks of dust off his suit. She dare not stop. If she did the reality of what was happening would break her spirit. Time enough to grieve later, in private.

'Do ye have everything with you Conor?'

'I do Mam, for goodness sake how many times are you going to ask me!'

There wasn't much to put in the bag he carried and he was embarrassed that she had packed a sod of turf for him to take to America with him. She never had much to give but she knew instinctively the small things that mattered: a Hospital Sweeps ticket as a gift for weddings, a shamrock from the sod ditch below in the field for St. Patrick's Day.

'You'll see when you get out there, Conor. Your relations will be delighted with a little bit of home. You can get a bottle of whiskey at Shannon as well.'

'Mam! For God's sake, a turf, I'll be a laughing stock when I get over there! I have to go now. Uncle Patrick is waiting for me in the car outside. Goodbye Mam, I have to go.'

She stopped fussing, looked him in the face, gathered her strength to hold him to her breast for one last time.

'Goodbye son, make us proud of you,' she said fondly giving him a big kiss. He never liked this kissing business and always wiped the moistness off his face as quickly and as unobtrusively as he could. This morning he didn't.

His father sat in the chimney corner on a battered old cushionless arm chair, an *eadaill* that was among the many items he had recovered from the sea many years ago. He looked smaller today, Conor thought as he walked across the stone flagged kitchen floor towards him. Not the imposing figure that had dominated his childhood; that lived by the maxim 'Spare the rod and spoil the child.' Dressed in his work dungarees, work worn hands clasped in his lap, now he looked ahead in a kind of silent daze. All his life's expectations were built around Conor taking over the farm from him, as he had done in his time. Used to being the authority figure in the household the realisation that he was not in control of the family's destiny anymore was overwhelming, a turn of events too devastating to take in.

He looked up at his son: 'Good luck Conor, God be with you,' he managed

'Good bye Dad, take care of yourself.'

That was all.

Conor lifted his travel bag. His mother standing at the door dipped her fingers in the holy water font and splashed a drop on him:

'Here, bless yourself son, we'll miss you.'

The car moved slowly off the street, and suddenly a terrible outburst of crying was heard. Unable to contain herself any longer his mother, in an extremity of grief, threw herself across the bonnet of the car:

'Conor, Conor, oh Conor my child' she cried, 'what will we do at all, what will we do without you!'

Conor was visibly shocked and upset. His mother's unexpected display of anguish, her terror stricken expression, brought it home to him, for the first time, the calamity that had befallen the family. For the first time since he planned to leave he felt responsible and tears stung his eyes as his mother fell back helplessly from the moving car. It was too late now. Too late. Looking through the rear window he watched her clutch her hair and tear her apron in an agony of grief. Her wild keening grew fainter as the car picked up speed. Soon the little thatched, whitewashed house with its purple and red fuchsia hedge, its hay ricks and tiny knot of neighbours waving farewell, faded and disappeared as the car turned through a bend in the road.

ಎ

In the army men became clockwork toys: they marched together, ate together — they even shat together. There was no privacy. If there is anything more certain to break down vanity or conceit it is to sit, cheek to cheek as it were, on a long row of unpartitioned toilet bowls placed in an open room. Here everyone, brothers in embarrassment sat enthroned: farm boys and city slickers, Rednecks and Yankees, Hoosiers and Okies — plus a sprinkling of immigrants. Black, white and brown defecated together, farted together, wiped together. Diarrhoetic or constipated, shy or brash, noisy or silent, nothing was hidden. What had previously been that most private of functions, going to the toilet, was performed in this open, communal room.

Showers too were taken in full display. Black, brown and white, big and small, soaped, rubbed and scrubbed at a row of showerheads fixed to the wall where nothing was concealed. Conor's Uncle Ellis, a round, chubby man with an elfin grin wasn't slow to remind him of what was in store:

'Hey Conor!' he would chuckle at family gatherings or when his neighbours, the Frediricis, came over to visit. 'When you go down there to basic training you better not bend down to pick up the soap if you drop it in the shower.'

This caused great amusement — to everyone but Conor. Not indeed that there was anything to fear as the male member tends to shrink from such public scrutiny.

The toilets, the haircuts, the bullying, the showers: this was all part of a well devised construct of Empire designed to break down the individual. Small things amounting to an entirety that would make unquestioning killers of law abiding citizens; produce robots that would reflexively obey orders without question. While all traces of individuality were diminished a fresh pride would be implanted in the new 'family' and its various units: platoon, company, battalion or regiment. 'We are the Ultimate Weapon' was instilled in the recruits brain. Regardless of technology or weapons development, nuclear or conventional, they were the 'ultimate weapons' that would eventually have to be deployed on the ground. They were special, they were indispensable, they were the defenders of their country. A proud boast indeed.

On parade he took no pride in the American flag fluttering from the mast: after all it wasn't his flag. But what could he do? He was trapped. So he marched and trained, learned to 'field strip' and reassemble the 'M14 air cooled, gas operated, magazine fed shoulder weapon'.

'Your weapon is your life, it is your new girl friend, you sleep with it, you eat with it, you kill with it, it never leaves your sight' was the mantra the instructor drummed into them time and time again.

On the firing range Conor learned to shoot from standing, kneeling and lying positions, becoming so proficient that he soon earned the 'expert' medal for accuracy.

He trained with hand grenades, rocket launchers and threw himself into the gory bayonet practice.

'The bayonet fighter's positions are guard, short guard, and high port. He executes the following movements: whirl, long thrust, short thrust, withdrawal, parry right and left, vertical and horizontal butt strokes, smash and slash hitting the junction of neck and shoulder or the head throat and arms.'

'What is the spirit of the bayonet!'

'KILL. KILL, KILL.

Practise charges were made yelling and screaming at stuffed, simulated human figures.

'When the bayonet penetrates a body the blade is driven in to the hilt and then twisted to effect the greatest possible damage. With maximum penetration,' the instructor explained, 'the blade can be difficult to withdraw so you place your boot on the enemy's chest to facilitate withdrawal.'

These murderous practices imparted so casually as a preparation for the 'killing fields' were a long way from the gentle pastures and pastoral pursuits of Conor's previous life — and all for a meagre pay cheque of $78.00 dollars a month.

$78.00 dollars!

Was it for this he had fled?

And still he could see no way out.

'Mail call' was always greeted with keen anticipation. A break from the rigid discipline. News from home.

*Dear Conor,*

*We are all well here as I hope this finds you. The weather is turning cold and soon we'll have to house the cattle again. Your father is making the best of things but with so many people emigrating from here it is very hard to find help. We have enough hay saved so we should be alright for the winter. Dad misses you but he is determined to hold out till you get back. Sometimes he is very depressed and it is hard to get him out of it. When he is talking to the neighbours he always keeps his best side out and they are always asking for you.*

*Patrick Kielty was in here the other day. He was drawing water from our well for the cattle as usual. He was perished with the cold so I made him a cup of tea and you should have seen the drop from his nose! You wouldn't want to be drinking out of the same cup!! Things isn't so good in America says he to me. Oh aye, there's a depression there and a lot of people out of work. I was reading it in the paper. The bloody cheek of him, so I went up to the room and got the cheque you sent us before you went in the army and showed it to him. Does that look like a depression says I, and I'll tell you that took the talk off him. You know what I always say Conor, you have to keep your heart up if your belly was trailing the ground, ha ha. Well I'll finish now and please write soon and tell us how you are getting on in your new life. We know you don't like the army but sure you won't find the time going in till we're all back together again, write soon we love to hear from you.*

*Your fond mother, Catherine*

Much as he looked forward to these letters they always made Conor homesick: An overwhelming nausea in the pit of his stomach; a dreadful longing mingled with a physical sickness that permeated every fibre of his being, crying out for the familiar fields and friends of home.

But there was no time for self pity. Army life went on impervious to sentiment, basic training was coming to an end and only the night infiltration course to be completed. When it came it was worse even than the most vivid descriptions he had heard. The rain poured down on the open trucks that conveyed them to the range; it trickled off their steel helmets on to their ponchos; penetrating to the skin it dripped and flowed in little rivulets down the steel floor of the truck where they hunkered. Dropped off at the edge of a field in complete darkness they were immediately immersed in a living hell of mud, gunfire and explosions. Although well prepared for this ordeal no words could match what he saw. Waiting at the edge of the range with the other members of his platoon his heart whacked against his chest at what he saw.

The Sergeant in charge had seen it all before: 'Right you pantywaist motherfukkers, let's see who the pussies are and who's got a pair:

'Fall In!'
'Move, move, move it!'
'Tensh Hut!'
'Right Dress.'
'High port arms,
'Forward Harch'

'DOUBLE TIME, OVER THE TOP...

'Now... On your bellies, crawl, you put your fucking chicken head up you lose it. What we got here is live rounds. Stand up, you die. Kiss the dirt! Go! Go! Go!'

Conor threw himself down in the muck. Holding his rifle across his forearms to keep it out of the mud he crawled forward under a maze of barbwire. Heavy machinegun fire from several positions sent tracer bullets, fiery red streaks of orange-red light, over their heads. RAT-A-TAT-TAT. Bright as meteorites they blazed in deadly streaks across the field. RAT-A-TAT-TAT. Like Mad Sweeney in the Battle of Magh Rath his fear was turning gradually to a kind of mad exhilaration. But he would not flee This was everything for which he had been trained. Made pitch perfect.

KABOOM!

An explosion erupted beside him throwing dirt and sandbags in the air, the flash illuminating the dirty, smoke filled night sky. 'Artillery rounds coming in', he thought, but still he wasn't afraid. Dirt and mud and the acrid smell of explosives. He started to scream defiance. One of his comrades shouted for help in the darkness behind him. He had lost his nerve and become entangled in the wire. Conor shouted for a medic but redoubled his own efforts to get to the end.

'Gas, gas, gas, gas,' the shout went up, and he saw a blue-grey haze of CS gas drifting across the field, stinging his eyes. Donning his gas mask he blew the acrid stench out as he had been taught and went on. Another comrade, too slow in putting the mask on shouted for a medic as he staggered, blinded and gasping for breath through the barb wire. Another explosion went off ahead and to his right. In the light of the flash he could see the scene silhouetted as in a nightmare. Smoke drifted across the range. And the rain poured down. This was a piece of cake. He had heard of people losing their head in the noise, dirt and confusion, standing up to run and being cut down by machine gun fire. He laughed. There was nothing to be afraid of if you kept your head down and kept going. And so he did. Hard labour on the farm had made him a lot tougher than these city boys. Scrabble forward with your elbows, then knees forward one at a time, like a worm, or a snake, keep the rifle clean. Inch by inch, piece of cake, keep going, he was immune to bullets, mortars or explosives. We are the Ultimate Weapons.

The sergeant was waiting for them:

'Alright, on your feet. Now! Get up, up, move out! Up, up you fucking panty waists! On the trucks. Move it out. White glove inspection at 0100 hours. Move it!'

Covered with dirt from head to toe, sweating and freezing all at the same time, Conor pulled himself off the ground. It was over! He had come through a fiery rite of passage and emerged whole and unscathed. The passing out parade that followed was an event of great pride for him. Finally he was indeed the invincible 'Ultimate Weapon'. Events moved quickly and days later his company was dispersed to army posts all over the U.S., and he to Fort Lewis, Washington, to join the 4th Infantry Division.

The letters he sent home now were watermarked with

colourful images of infantrymen and tanks charging into battle. Mentally and physically he was becoming further and further removed from the life he had left behind in Killawaddy'. Now he was thoroughly absorbed into this great monolithic giant with many faces and no face; where you were something and you were nothing, a small but vital link in a chain that stretched all the way to the Commander in Chief in the White House — where final life and death decisions were made for these disposable 'Ultimate Weapons'.

*September 8th 1962*
*Dear Mam and Dad,*
*I hope you are both keeping well. Thanks for all your letters with news of home and sorry for not writing sooner. As you know from my last letter I have been assigned to an infantry division here in Washington. Army life agrees well with me and if all goes well I expect to be promoted through the ranks.*

*There are people here from all over America. What a strange assortment. John Taylor a hillbilly from Cornhills Missouri, wears cowboy boots and plays country and western music all day, a pueblo Indian from New Mexico doesn't shave, he pulls his beard out once every three weeks, there's a black man, as black as coal swears he's Irish! His name is Mclemore but he sure aint from Conemara! The sergeant came in one day and ordered the blacks and whites to mix as the blacks were one end of the barrack and the whites at the other end. When I come back here, he said, I want to see every other bunk black and white. Everyone was grumbling because some had the floor spit-shined in their spot but they had to move anyway. As well as that people wanted to be beside their buddies. A week later they were all back again where they were before and that was the end of that 'integration' experiment.*

*There's some of our fellows here getting sent overseas under secret orders. Of course there's nothing secret in the army and the rumours are that they're being sent to Vietnam. Nobody rightly knows where it is but it seems they are being sent out to fight the communists in IndoChina. It's all very secret. I'm not sure how I feel about it but there's extra money if you do get sent out and that would be very welcome.*

*Sorry to hear you're not keeping well Dad and hope you get better soon. I know you're working too hard as always so I hope the money I send helps out with the bills. Mam says you had to sell some of the cattle but I hope you can keep going. Hard to believe it's fourteen months since I left! Things haven't gone according to plan and the money isn't big here in the army. However if I get promotion I'll get more money so I'm doing my best. They say promotion comes quicker overseas so if I get a chance I'll go. I have to put in my time so might as well make the best of it.*

*Love, Conor*

Torn between a desire to help his parents and his growing attraction to army life Conor was full of conflicting emotions. What should he do? His parents needed him at home. They were struggling desperately to manage without him. He felt guilty at abandoning them. Yet, to desert the army and go home was unthinkable. Even if he was prepared to do that he didn't have enough money saved to make a difference on the farm. Far from it! His small wage was hardly enough even for himself. By the middle of the month he was skint!

On the other hand if he managed to complete his time he should get a good job when he came out in recognition of his service to the U.S. Then he could send enough money home to make a difference, or indeed save enough to go home for good. He envied his American comrades who didn't have to cope with such dilemmas. But what was the point in confiding in them! It was no use. They wouldn't understand, or care. For them it was a career choice, or they had family support if it wasn't.

In the lower ranks thinking isn't required, or encouraged! The 'chain of command' takes care of that. Matters were taken out of his hands when transfer orders came through on 25th of September 1966 for his Division to be deployed to Camp Holloway in Pleiku, northwest of Saigon in Vietnam. The Americans had established an armed presence there long before admitting any armed intervention in the region. The Viet Cong attack on this strategic base in the previous year was one of the key events that had drawn the Americans into an escalation of the conflict.

On arrival at Camp Holloway Conor's unit was immediately thrown into 'Operation Attleboro' a 'search and destroy' operation by the 196th Light Infantry Brigade in Tay Ninh province designed to disrupt or eradicate Viet Cong (VC) supply lines. Densely forested, the terrain also had large, open expanses of savannah and elephant grass, the latter ranging from waist high to over six feet: perfect cover for an ambush.

The American assault, under overall command of General de Saussere, began at daybreak as four columns of infantry fanned out from open country to enter the tree line. As they advanced the men carried their weapons proudly, bragged to each other about the army's capabilities, became more spirited as they went: How many gooks would they kill today? Fucking wogs in this shithole country. The quicker they got it over with and went home to the 'real world' the better.

No training could prepare a man for actual combat and they were in for a shock. Faced with the possibility of actual battle — kill or be killed himself — Conor realizes he doesn't really know, regardless of his training, how he'll react: will he fight courageously, will he run away; can he actually kill another human being when it comes right down to it? An individual that has done him no harm? It is he that is the stranger, the belligerent, in their country This is not his land, nor this his fight. His father fought with the I.R.A. in Dublin in the Easter Rebellion of 1916 against overwhelming odds, but that was different, he was fighting a hostile enemy, defending his own country; maybe even just like the Viet Cong were doing in the bush ahead of him now. Dare he even think it!

Turning to his buddy, Leo, that he had befriended since he came to Vietnam he could see no fear or hesitance. Leo, a lanky good humoured six footer, with always a smile or a joke on his lips, was from a neighbouring village at home. With a similar background there was a natural affinity between the two.

'Well Leo, now's our chance for glory.' Conor said wryly, masking his fear with bravado and a smile he didn't feel. 'This is the real deal! What do you think of it, it's a long way from Clare to here!'

'Ah, to hell with it, Conor,! If ye worry ye die and if ye don't worry ye die. So why worry!'

'Well it's some Job's comforter you are! Aren't you afraid you might take off when the shooting starts. This is one hell of a place to die. Didn't you ever hear it said that he who turns and runs away will live to fight another day?'

'Conor me bucko, a coward dies a thousand deaths, a brave man dies but one! We'll get a purple heart out of this yet, or maybe even a Medal of Honour. When you get out of here and pull up to the home place in Killawaddy' with one of those yokes on your chest won't you be the right hero! Just think of it!'

'Shhhh, shhh, shush, look up ahead, they're there?'

'What?'

'Shhh!'

Conor thought he could see shapes flitting through the dense undergrowth further on.

'Look up ahead,' he whispered,' it's show time, down, down.'

Creeping stealthily forward they had gone barely a hundred metres when they were stopped dead in their tracks by Viet Cong guarding a well-camouflaged camp. Fierce fighting erupted immediately and in the blink of an eye; Conor's C Company commander, his first sergeant and six other soldiers lay dead. Twelve more were badly wounded. Reinforcements were called in and the medics began evacuating the injured. All bravado was now gone and in its place only panic, confusion and chaos. This was not going to be the walkover envisioned by the Americans.

Conor and his comrades were in the thick of it: the screams of the wounded, the lifeless staring eyes of the dead, the reek of gun smoke, the rapid clatter of automatic fire, the hum of rounds clipping through the leaves, the sickening thud when they smacked into a body; the smell of fear, the cloying, sickly smell of spilled guts that oozed and gurgled obscenely on to the ground.

All their lives were changed in an instant of nightmarish ferocity.

Darkness fell, the fighting waned and the character of this fierce collision between two equally determined forces emerged. The vegetation was so thick that American units easily became separated, losing their own unity and contact with other units. The American ace-in-the-hole, massive firepower, was largely nullified by fear of hitting their own people whose exact location could not be determined in the dense jungle. American casualties were mounting, mainly because of a skilful defence by the 9th Viet Cong Division's Reconnaissance Company commanded by a Colonel Cam.  The Viet Cong camp was well protected by camouflaged concrete bunkers, manned by determined machine gun crews. Well-concealed snipers high up in the larger trees, were picking off individual Americans with relative ease.

After a relatively quiet night, battalion commander Major Dickson launched a two-company flanking movement to the east. An hour later, hoping he had outflanked the enemy, he began an advance through the heavy undergrowth to the northeast and promptly ran into a battalion of North Vietnamese regulars manning bunkers. They engaged immediately and defenders and attackers' fire became deafening and intense. In some locations the two forces were battling it out only ten to twenty meters apart. Dickson called in artillery fire and directed two company-size flanking attacks. Both failed. Rifle and machine gun fire was so constant that merely to stand up invited a quick death.

Suddenly, the North Vietnamese began attacking in waves. Conor's Company defended as best they could but could neither attack nor withdraw without inviting prohibitive casualties. Except for one enlisted man, everyone in Dickson's command party including himself was wounded. With air or artillery support either ineffective or unwise because of the uncertain proximity of friendly forces, the only remaining option was to retreat or bring in more forces to get at the enemy flank and rear — or both.

The rescue force had already been selected. Late in the day, just after the third ferocious Viet Cong wave attack, A Company from the 2nd Battalion, 27th Infantry, was landed about 400 meters behind what was believed to be the enemy right flank. Almost immediately, the newcomers drew heavy fire from tree snipers and encountered a new deadly hazard: 'fire tunnels.' The defenders had chopped narrow firing lanes into tall elephant grass obscuring the open lanes below waist level. At the beginning of each tunnel was a bunker manned by a machine gun crew with a commanding view through the length of the tunnel cutting down anyone unknowingly stepping into the firing lane.

The 2nd Battalion's A Company commander was an early victim, and a half-hour later, the 2nd Battalion commander, who had accompanied the unit, was also killed. As with Dickson's's stymied forces, their rescuers found that they too were on the defensive, partly because they did not have enough able men to evacuate their many wounded and partly because of the fierceness of the Viet Cong defence.

Conor and Leo lay in a shallow depression in the ground. They were cut off from what was left of their platoon There was nowhere to go. Up ahead was teeming with Viet Cong, behind them C Company was suffering heavy casualties. They could neither advance nor retreat.

'It's a long way from Clare to here, Conor. What do you think?' Leo said smiling across his crooked smile.

'Jesus! It's a long way from Clare! Is that all you can think of to say at a time like this?'

'Might as well sing grief as cry it, Conor.'

'Here, take this.' Conor handed a small packet over to Leo. 'If we don't make it out of here I want you to take this to my parents.'

'Ah, don't be thinking like that, sure we'll get out of it! A Company are getting ready to mount an attack. But look I'll take it anyway, just in case'

A Company having laid down a base of supporting artillery fire pushed forward at a run. After advancing only thirty metres they ran into withering fire from two heavily fortified machine gun nests. Nothing could stand against the firepower of the VC armaments: AK-47s, the deadly Soviet made RPGs and the German made Schmeiser submachine guns. Once again the Americans were outgunned and outnumbered. It could only be a matter of minutes before the VC would press their advantage and launch an all out counter attack. Sheer force of numbers alone would allow them to overrun the American units.

Men pass through terror into courage, the quarry at bay forgets fear and fights for his very life. Victory was out of the question. Now it was nothing more than a matter of survival and getting out alive. He realises that he is only a small part of a much bigger whole, but small though that part might be, it is not insignificant. He would be his father's son and like his childhood heroes, Cathal Brugha and Dan Breen, face the overwhelming odds. With cunning and luck he might just be able to rescue his unit from inevitable defeat and annihilation.

'Leo! Better to die on our feet like men than be cut down like sheep. There's a shallow ravine running up the slope. Look. Over there to our right. There's two emplacements at the top that's holding everyone down. There's enough cover to get within attacking position. If we can take one out then that'll give us cover to take out the second one. If we stay here we'll all be slaughtered. It's worth the risk.'

Leo's ready banter had deserted him. Conor was right. They had to do it themselves.

'Okay then, I'll signal over to the other lads to put down a covering fire as a distraction. It just might work. I'm ready!'

When the barrage of supporting fire started the two men jumped from their position and scrambled low across the bullet swept ground to the shallow ravine that Conor had spotted.

Focussing on a clump of trees to the side of the enemy bunker they bounded and crawled as they had done in the night infiltration course in Fort Dix. Suddenly enfilading fire from a previously quiet VC machine gun position tore into the trees around them, sent up vicious little spurts of dirt from the ground. Then the .50-caliber machine gun supporting their attack jammed and went silent

Conor heard Leo grunt and looked around to see him fall to the ground with blood pumping out of a chest wound. He was dead before he hit the ground.

'Aw, Jesus Christ Leo, what happened?' Conor exclaimed going over to where his comrade had fallen. There was nothing he could do. He reached over, took his hand, and whispered an Act of Contrition in his ear:

'Oh my God I am heartily sorry for having offended thee... Rest in peace good friend.'

Finally he put the hand down. Reaching over he gently straightened his friends collar and rearranged the tattered edges of the uniform around the gaping chest wound.

'Bastards! Bastards!' he cried hitting the blood-soaked ground with his fists. Now this war was personal. They had killed his friend. He would go on. He must go on. He would avenge this death and save his comrades below from the slaughter.

Dashing from cover to cover he closed on the machine gun nest. There were four soldiers in it. They didn't see him till it was too late. He threw a grenade into the pit. It exploded throwing up a shower of dirt and bits of torn flesh. He finished them off with a burst of automatic fire. Once again as in Ft.

Dix, battle madness had taken hold of him and he felt nothing at these deaths, the mutilated bodies that normally would be abhorrent.

Two members of his platoon, seeing the engagement, now raced up the hill to support him.

We're going up the hill' he shouted when they came within hailing distance. 'Fix your bayonets. Follow me. Go for the wooded knoll.'

With fixed bayonets and rifles carried at high port, screaming as they ran, they reached the knoll under heavy fire and were immediately confronted with enemy foxholes. Lunging forward they tore into the first foxhole, bayonets foremost. The terror filled shrieks of the bayoneted soldiers rose above the din of battle. Conor threw a grenade into the second foxhole killing three of the occupants. One stunned survivor raised his rifle but before he could fire, with a savage thrust of his bayonet, Conor plunged the bloodstained blade through his chest.

He was now ahead of the other two men and racing towards the gun emplacement. A cluster of grenades thrown from further uphill exploded around him. Ignoring the danger, he charged headlong at an anti-tank gun firing point-blank at him. He could feel a stinging in his thigh where a piece of shrapnel from one of the grenades had hit. A warm trickle of blood coursed down his leg, drenching his fatigues. Ignoring the intense pain he continued his charge

'Come on boys, we're nearly there,' he shouted to the other men.

His senses were sharper than they had ever been. With

an intensity he had never felt before he was keenly aware of everything around him: each blade of grass, the rough bark of trees, the feverish enemy, the smell of battle, the explosions, the rattle of machine gun fire, the falling soldiers. A great euphoria came over him, he was invincible, enchanted, untouchable. Together they went on, screaming and yelling, firing from the hip, ripping and stabbing enemy flesh with their bayonets, throwing grenades into bunkers and foxholes.

A Viet Cong rushed at them screaming and firing as he went. Conor felt a blinding flash, the hammer blow of a hail of bullets. He was hit in the head and chest. Everything went into slow motion. A puff of pink mist sprayed from his head where the last bullet impacted. He spun around and fell to the ground. Limp. Folded like a puppet with the strings severed. The canopy of trees swirled around overhead. Around and around. Making him dizzy. The sounds of battle faded away. He was cold. Voices came to him as in a fog, far away.

*'Conor, Conor are you hit?'*

Blurred shapes hovered over him. His mouth opened, opened and shut and opened again. He struggled for words but they would not come. Blood poured from his ears, his mouth, his nose. No words came, only a strangled gurgle. He tried to hold his hands out but couldn't. He was surrounded by a red-tinged mist.

Ah now, there it was. The mist cleared and he could see who was there — and was shocked to see his mother smiling in the doorway beckoning to him to follow her:

'Conor, Conor, oh Conor my child,' she was saying. 'What

will we do at all, what will we do without you!'

He went inside and there in his favourite chair in the chimney corner, just as he had left him, was his father. He looked pale and gaunt:

'You see, I told you Conor, once you go you can never come home again.'

'But of course I can, Dad, I'm home, home at last' he said, putting his arms around both of them. 'We're together again.

# 3

# COSMOS

Shorter days and the consequent longer nights of Autumn left a good deal of free time for the inhabitants of Killawaddy. This was when 'ramblin' started — visits to neighbour's houses to chat, swap stories or play cards. These pleasant evenings of card playing and storytelling were sometimes subject to unexpected interruptions. The call to action always came from my father:

'C'mon, hurry up there, get them few wee jobs done and we'll make a lok of ropes tonight.'

The summons always came as a surprise to me. With hindsight I'm sure the plan was gestating in his mind for some time beforehand but he was a reserved sort of man who kept himself to himself. Doubtless the position of the planets and other celestial signs, sunsets, sunrise, cloud formations, bird behaviour, etc, were noted quietly long before that. These signs in the heavens told the astute countryman, long before his senses were dulled by Met Eirinn, what the weather had in store. His deliberations, when finally arrived at, were not at all democratic in any sense of them being a decision in consultation with the family, or with his primary partner in the enterprise: me!

No!

Perversely, and for some reason known only to himself he regarded rope-making as a nocturnal occupation. Service was compulsory. Without any preamble he picked calm, clear, moonlit nights for the job. His notions hardly ever coincided with mine and when the call came my plan for an evening of card-playing, already made, was doomed to disappointment. Experience told me there was no use in pleading, at least not with him, so I immediately appealed to my mother's sense of fairness. She could usually be got around when my father was unmoving. This almost always annoyed him who felt his authority was being undermined by the popular decision of my mother's court of appeal which judgement nearly always was:

'Ah, sure what harm is he doing, why don't you let the young fella go ahead. Ye can't put an old head on young shoulders y'know.'

Nearly always.

My mother's decision had to be finely balanced and modified by such diplomatic considerations as: what humour is he in?

This time my appeal was fruitless. The decision of the court was:

'I'm afraid ye'll have to talk to yer father about that.'

Making ropes is an occupation that, over the years, became very familiar to me. This is not the kind of rope that, for the modern reader, may immediately spring to mind. It is not any kind of cord or line we see anymore but concerns a product and craft that is now lost: the making of hay and straw ropes. The technique did not, as so many have, die of neglect; with the advent of affluence, mechanised farming and baling twine, there was just no need for it anymore. It is a relic of a simpler past where necessity, as well as a critical shortage of cash, being the mother of invention, indigenous materials were used wherever possible.

We may list rope-making alongside those skills, now useless, that country people learned of necessity in their adolescence. It was as well-known to us as the iphone is to the youngsters of today —only not nearly as much fun. No indeed. It was hard, unrewarding, tedious work. Materials came from what the farmer had to hand: usually hay, straw or 'spret'. Spret was a kind of coarse, tough meadow grass that grew in wet land. It made poor feeding for cattle but excellent ropes.

Although an unpretentious and simple craft of the Irish countryside we may justifiably boast that it inspired the literary classes: In *The Twisting of the Rope* from *Tales of Red Hanrahan* W.B. Yeats tells of a humorous incident during which Hanrahan was tricked by the woman of the house where he was a guest — but more of that later.

Making ropes was a big step in preparation for the eventful day when the rick or haystack was made. At least two big balls, known as clews, of these straw ropes had to be made prior to the big day. On the chosen evening the sheaves were brought in and the ends beaten thoroughly with a heavy wooden mallet to make the straw, always oaten, even more flexible. At sowing time the previous spring this oats was sown more thickly so as to be thinner and finer in texture. Thus prepared it was now thrown at the back door where my father squatted on a low stool ready to commence operations. His agile fingers plied and fed the straw to my thraw-hook or twister. He teased and coaxed the yellow skeins through his expert hands as I twisted it around and around into a tough, slender *súgán*, slowly inching my way backwards out of the kitchen, out the front door (left open for that purpose) and across the road to Dowdican's house which was opposite ours.

This was not a job that challenged the mind or mechanical abilities of the twister. In fact it was one of the most boring jobs on earth. The only qualification required was one of infinite patience. If patience was not a natural attribute of the twister then threats of retribution and the infliction of pain encouraged the acquisition of it very speedily. While my father might gain some satisfaction from compliments paid him by visitors on his abilities as a rope maker, there were no such accolades for the twister who, although essential to the operation, required no skill. As the rope lengthened I moved slowly backwards through the friendly pool of yellow light that fell from the front door, out the cobbled street and on into the darkness beyond.

'Great night for the job', neighbours might say as they came and went to the house. 'Begod, there's no one can make ropes with yer father. He can turn his hands to anything.'

And indeed he could! It took years of practise to turn out a product of uniform thickness. A good rope maker made a product that was strong, but slender too. The weave had to be just right: too loose and it unravelled, too tight and it broke. A thick rope made an unnecessarily bulky, heavy clew; too thin and that too would break under pressure. Three quarters of an inch in diameter was about right.

Twisting was a painstakingly slow procedure as the rope gradually and tediously lengthened across the road. Attempts at increasing the pace did no good. All it achieved was to annoy my father who just got irritated and barked at me to slow down. Feeding the straw to the twist could not be hurried, it was a careful and deliberate process.

On mild nights when Dowdican's front door was open, and my father not paying attention, the monotony was broken by stealing a bit further and twisting the rope longer and longer through their kitchen and on out to their back door. Cattie, the woman of the house, who usually sat contented on a 'furm' by the fireside, didn't mind at all. My father disapproved of this intrusion as an unwarranted imposition on the neighbours. I was supposed to jerk on the rope, a kind of semaphore, before I got to the house as a signal that it was time to coil the freshly made length on to the clew. In this home grown semaphore one jerk from him meant: 'you're going too fast; two might mean: 'Slow down, I'm getting annoyed now', and so on.

'Why didn't ye tell me ye were gone that far?' he would growl when he realised I had exceeded my remit, but sometimes there was a hint of humour in his voice, perhaps remembering his own impetuous younger days. I don't know. I didn't think to ask and he never told me.

Cattie's son Eugene was a different kettle of fish. I had mixed feelings about him.

Having no 'wirelesss' in our own home visiting their house that had, was a great thrill. My trips twice a week to their kitchen to listen to the serial thriller, 'Perry Mason', were discouraged by him and I felt uncomfortable under his critical gaze. The Perry Mason hour was one of those cliff-hanger series that left the listener wondering at the end of each episode how the hero was ever going to survive against terrible odds. Once, in a fit of pique, he put the Phillips wireless out of adjustment, claiming that the 'trickel' was broken. I was devastated at the news of the malfunctioning 'trickel'. It was a matter of life and death to a young mind to find out if Perry was going to outwit the criminal in his usual clever way, or if this was the time that crime was going to triumph over good. I had to know. Mind whirling, I sat there desperately seeking a solution.

In contemplation of the unthinkable mechanical breakdown a melancholy silence descended on the kitchen. Things brightened up when Eugene gathered up the tin cans and went out to the byre to milk the cows. I looked at Cattie in despair:

'Mrs. Dowdican do you mind if I try and fix the trickel please?'

'Eugene'll be very cross with you if you break it,' she reasoned.

'But it's broke already Mrs. Dowdican and I'll be very careful. I think I know what might be wrong with it,' I lied.

'Well alright then go ahead but be careful because if he comes in and gets you rooting at it we're both in for it!'

I fiddled with the knobs, pressing and turning. It was no good. Then I noticed little levers at the base of the knobs and thought: what harm would it do to move them. I did, and soon Perry Mason's voice resonated through the kitchen. Cattie chuckled and poking the fire put a few more sods on. I listened enthralled as the plot unfolded.

After awhile Eugene came in from his work and I told him with some satisfaction and pride of how I had fixed the 'trickel'. After all, for a young lad with no training whatsoever it was quite an accomplishment. Giving me a sour look, his reaction of annoyance rather than delight at the good news was puzzling. Cattie said nothing. She looked at me with merry eyes and laughed, all her folds shaking, and I didn't understand what was so funny for a long time.

ও

These frosty, calm nights magnified the plaintive conversation of the swans on Bunduff lake, giving the sad-sweet notes a melancholy unworldly expression. It carried to me, sing-song, swan-songed, on the frosty air; unearthly music that wafted and fell gently from the sky as the graceful guardians of the lake kept their lonely vigil. So sang the children of King Lir sent on a nine hundred year exile by their witch stepmother, Oife, when she turned them into four swans. Regretting what she had done, and unable to recant the spell, she gave them the power that, 'there shall be no music in the world equal to yours, the plaintive music you shall sing'.

And indeed I have never heard music to match the bewitching beauty of swan song carried on the still air of a cold and starry night.

During the long, monotonous, repetitive journeys between our front door and the door of the house across the road I twisted around, and around, and around. A study of the star studded sky overhead was the only way of relieving the tedium. There wasn't much else to do. The incandescent complexity of the Milky Way, Orion Nebula, the Plough; as the years went by, I knew them well. My mind grappled unsuccessfully, as it still does, with the magnitude and vastness of space. From the enveloping inky blackness mantling the Earth I looked up at the vast never-ending cascade of shimmering light and wondered.

Could it be true that some of these bright stars in the heavens, giant supernovas, had ceased to exist long years before? Only their twinkling images that had been travelling at the speed of light, an unbelievable 186,000 miles per second, now reached us over vast expanses of empty space, hundreds of years after the star's destruction in a cataclysmic inferno. We could see them and yet they had long ago exploded into atoms! Some had flared into brilliance, lived and died long before the earth came into being. And, incredibly, we were there, in a different shape then — ethereal particles floating in the cosmos. We are formed of the very stardust, molecules and atoms reconstructed by cosmic evolution from the gas and residue of supernovae. And chance assembled us here. An accident almost. A different drifting of atoms and we might have been one of those bright stars in other, grimmer skies. And the earth too will vanish. It will self-destruct in a catastrophic Armageddon some billions of years from now; burned to a crisp or swallowed by our dying sun. A wicked, malfunctioning sun that will become a Red Giant, then a White Dwarf and eventually a dead and lifeless entity. Other stars and galaxies will come into being, formed of our atoms, and they will know nothing of us, our civilisation, or a place once called Earth! A great Cosmic Recycling. And will other humans grow there formed in our image and likeness on another earthlike planet and in the image of God the Creator? We in Him and Him in us? Or are we creatures in His dream? Is nothing real? Is it true that for space travellers time stops as they approach the speed of light and keeps them forever young? How can it be possible that in our overriding conceit and pomposity our sun, and yes, our entire solar system is only an insignificant entity in an obscure corner of that myriad, luminescent mass of stars and light, a galaxy we call the Milky Way? The Milky Way itself lost and tiny in the immensity of never-ending space. Did not God create us and is not everything else in the universe secondary to our existence? Black holes? Invisible objects in space weighing ten times more than the sun and collapsed into a volume the size of a football field; their gravity so immense that not even light can escape their pull. Enter there if you can, if you dare, and emerge somewhere else in space, somewhere else in time. The enigma of space travel. Could black holes serve as time machines carrying us to the distant past or the unknown future? This was 1961. How interesting it would be if I could take flight and re-emerge in the time of, say, Cathal Mór of the Wine-Red Hand and walk entranced:

> *'Through a land of Morn:*
> *The sun, with wondrous excess of light,*
> *Shone down and glanced*
> *Over seas of corn*
> *And lustrous gardens aleft and right.*

*Even in the clime*
*Of resplendent Spain,*
*Beams no such sun upon such a land;*
*But it was the time,*
*'Twas in the reign,*
*Of Cahal Mór of the Wine-red Hand...'* [1]

If I could travel backwards in time and kill my father or mother would I be born anyway? If there was life out there on other planets among the myriad stars were there other young people up there on one of those pinpricks of light, in a parallel existence, twisting ropes too? Their glow the light of a planet that burned out many years ago; an illumination that is still travelling even though the source has vanished; it's people unremembered and unrecorded. Parallel universes? Red giants? White dwarfs? Novae? Supernovae? Neutron stars? Neutrinos? Quarks and quasars and — three sharp jerks on the rope:

'Would ye slow down t'hell outa that willye!' my father shouted in exasperation.

My space wandering, colliding with his concern for more immediate earthbound things, crashed to Earth.

Any preoccupation with the heavens was not going to be allowed to interfere with his reputation as a ropemaker, or his output for the night. A well-made rope would serve better in the coming storms than any starry eyed contemplation of the mysteries of the night sky.

[1] King Cahal Mór of the Wine-Red Hand (A vision of Connacht in the Thirteenth Century), James Clarence Mangan

Northwards, in the direction of the vast Arctic wastes, barrages of luminescence shot skywards. Travelling at the speed of light, long luminous curtains of fire painted a majestic, rapidly shifting backdrop to the canopy of stars. Shimmering draperies of pulsing brightness swept the contours of the abyss.

'Borey Dancers' the Kerry people called the display. We called it the Northern Lights. The older people sometimes watched and marvelled with us at this 'murmuring of the solar wind'. They believed the effect was created by sunlight reflected from the ice and snow of the frozen plains of the Arctic. One of our neighbours, Michael, had been to America, and consequently knew everything. 'That's the Rory Bory Alice', he said with a knowledgeable air, but few believed him, thinking it another one of his many fanciful concoctions. But Michael was right and indeed it was the Aurora Borealis, in Norse mythology identified with the ride of the Valkyries. My feet might have been fixed to the ground on those lonely, starry nights, but in my mind I was elsewhere, and rode across the bright speckled sky with those Norse warriors who rushed into the melee of battle selecting those whose fate it was to die.

> 'An chaor aduaidh:-
> olagón bog na cruinneas casadh ar a fearsad:
> sioscadh na gaoithe grianda
> os cionn folús an duibheagáin;
> dán mascalach an domhain, a phaidir gheal, ag soilsiú an
> mhaighnéadasféir...' [2]

[2] 'The northern fireball:- the soft wailing of the world, turning on its axis: the murmuring of the solar wind, over the vacuum of the abyss... An Chaor Aduaidh, Nuala Ní Dhomhnaill

On such clear starclustered nights, from the dark outline of the Bluestack mountains of Donegal, the faraway St. John's Point lighthouse winked at me like an earthbound star — a bright jewel of hope glistening in the dark, a shining beacon of life and hope for souls a-wander at sea. Further out along the ocean where *Sliabh Líag* sloped into the sea, Rathlin O'Beirne lighthouse, another watchful sentinel of the night, conversed busily in answering flashes with St. John's Point. Beside the byres, ramparted turfstacks stood silhouetted against a luminous sky. Arrayed up and down our little stony road the bright lamplit windows, starlit windows, strung under bushy-browed, thatched eaves, reflected the lamp-strewn canopy overhead.

Inside, gathered around the fireside, the old *seanchais*, their gnarled wise old heads lit by the dancing flames, told their stories. There was one to match every occasion. Rope twisting was another opportunity to pass on the old stories and entertain the listener. A good *seanchaí* gripped the attention of everyone present. Younger listeners would, in time, retell the tales etched on their minds on these long winter nights.

ॐ

How 'Red Willie' got rid of the tinker was a favourite and people often wondered if this was where W.B. Yeats got his inspiration for the Hanrahan story. Sure he could have! Wasn't he always going about the countryside asking questions? And wasn't he one with them in praising the Good People, the fairy folk of the hills and glens, the vanquished *Tuatha De Danaan*.

In *The Twisting of the Rope* from *Tales of Red Hanrahan* Yeats tells of how Hanrahan was tricked by the woman of the house where he was a guest. As the night wore on the poet became drunken and obstreperous so the clever woman hit on a plan. She got Hanrahan to twist a rope. As the rope lengthened he moved backwards step by step until he found himself outside the door. The woman immediately made a rush and slammed and bolted the door on him.

'Well that Yeats fella told a good story,' Tommy Fowley declared, 'but ye know it wasn't like that at all!

He was addressing the few ramblers that had strayed in, and my father at the bottom of the kitchen, wedged in between the dresser and the back door, busy turning wisps of straw into ropes.

' How is that?' my father said.

He knew well how it was but the retelling of it would while away the time, and anyway Tommy enjoyed having an audience.

'Well, this fellow, Willie Mc Gloin, was a bachelor and a returned Yank. He lived alone in a wee, thatched house down there by the Duff river on the borders of Sligo and Leitrim. Willie was fond of rambling to this house and that and one night when he came home what did he find but a travelling man, a tinker y'know, sitting by the fire. The night had turned bad and he had taken the liberty of going into the house for shelter...'

As the story unfolded it turned out that Willie didn't like the looks of the man. Not one bit. He was afraid but tried not to show it. Thinking discretion the better part of valour, however, he chatted away as casually as he could. He didn't like to insult or anger the man by asking him to leave so he made him a cup of tea while all the time fervently hoping he would leave of his own accord. The night grew wilder, the wind roared in the chimney and the tinker, oblivious to it all, was at his ease sitting by the fire. They chatted on, and on, and on. Willie's concern increased but still he said nothing. When it got into the early hours of the morning and still no sign of the visitor leaving, Willie, desperate by now, hit on a plan. He offhandedly suggested to the tinker that they should make a hay rope to secure the rick outside in the haggard.

'Shocking night out,' he ventured, 'That wind is still getting up. I'm afraid of me life the old hayrick is bound to get knocked if I don't tie it down. I'd be greatly obliged if ye'd give me a hand to twist a rope would ye?'

The man was grumpy about it but much to Willie's relief he agreed. Fetching an armful of hay and a thraw-hook the two men commenced to make the rope. Willie fed the hay from a corner of the kitchen while the visitor twisted on down the kitchen floor, out the door and on to the street. When he got him outside Willie jumped up, slammed shut the door and bolted it as fast as he could. Quenching the lamp he went off to his bed leaving the surprised stranger out in the cold.

'And that,' Tommy finished triumphantly, 'is the facts of where the great W.B. Yeats got his story about Hanrahan and *The Twisting of the Rope* — from our own man out the road there, Red Willie, and the clever way he got rid of his unwelcome visitor.

# 4

## THE BITTER SEASONS

My first memory of farm life is only indirectly related to it. Indirect in that the earliest recollection I have is of the bedroom door swinging open to a clanking of milk cans. It was my parents with a stern warning to my brother and I to behave until they got back from the fields.

But of course we would, and two pairs of angelic eyes looking back from the blankets was enough to convince the trusting but gullible pair that all was well. Maybe so, but foremost in our wily young minds was that they would be absent long enough for us to go on the prowl for what adventures might be found in the kitchen. The cows were out in the pasture fields, would take some time to milk, time enough for a successful raid. Their footsteps faded away down the lane and:

'Are they gone?'

'I think they are!

'You go and get it.'

'No, it's your turn.'

'It's not, I did it yesterday.'

'You're a coward!'

'No, I'm not!'

'Well go and get it then!'

A coward! Me! Being the oldest and branded a coward, even at such a young age, was a spur to action. I padded down to the kitchen in bare feet hopping from one to the other on the cold flagstones to see what goodies could be found. The sugar bowl was the main prize and sure enough there it was sitting in the middle of the table like Eve's apple or the first fruit of Harvest. The modus operandi had graduated from the simple taking of a spoon of sugar to a more precocious dipping of a slice of bread into the milk jug and then into the sugar bowl where half the sugar in the bowl stuck to the soppy bread.

The crime, of course, was soon detected and when it was we got off with nothing more than a good scolding and a threat of worse to come if it happened again. It did however have a sequel in the confession box down in the chapel where it formed the core of a good confession for many years to come, along with that other old reliable: 'taking the name of the Lord in vain.'

Well, you had to have something to confess, and I never heard of a penitent going into the confession box yet with nothing on his mind! These were easy peccadilloes to own up to. They were minor enough and fell into the lesser category of 'venial' where eternal damnation wasn't a consequence.

Venial was one of two classifications of sin defined by the Catholic Church and hammered into us by the nuns. The other was the more serious 'mortal' sin. This progression would come later with adolescence and the tussling with pubescent compulsions and faltering assimilation into the temptations and pitfalls of budding adulthood. Even then those two venial sins could be retained to serve as a preamble to summoning the courage to confess to more progressive offences. A subterfuge, a sort of shoe-horning or easing into the more serious stuff such as impure thoughts — and if you got lucky enough: acts. Sins of the flesh were always marked out for special attention. If you could schmooze the priest with the first couple of handy sins, something that wouldn't unduly ruffle his clerical feathers, you might be able to slide by unnoticed with the rest.

ಎ

With age comes care and these carefree days of lie-ins and sugar fests too soon became a thing of the past. Responsibility was ushered in with small jobs and it soon became my duty to be first up in the winter mornings to kindle the fire and boil the kettle for breakfast. The 'flame that never died' was 'raked', covered over with ashes every night and kindled back to life every morning.

Raking was done by smothering the live coals with ashes the night before and placing a few sods around that would catch alight and smoulder till morning. This preserved live coals until a new fire was lit from the embers.

Accordingly the hearth fire was kept alive for generations, as long as the house stood, without ever going out. Some of our neighbours placed the tongs crossways in front of the fire in the belief that iron had special properties that would prevent flame from passing it.

As an added protection the divine powers were invoked with a prayer:

> *Coiglimse an tine seo mar a choiglionns cach,*
> *Brid ina bun agus Muire ina barr;*
> *Dha aingle deag d'aingle na ngrast,*
> Ag cumhdach mo thi-sa go la.[3]

On moving house coals were taken to start the new fire thereby preserving the continuity. When the sole surviving member of a family passed away thoughtful neighbours took home a live coal from the last fire in the deceased's home and raked it with their own. In this way the dead family's fire was perpetuated and integrated with a living fire thereby entwining the spirits of both families.

Such thoughts did not concern me all those years ago in the cold and shivering mornings when I hunkered down to build the turf sods around the live embers, fanning sparks into life. Now I see it as the true eternal flame of the Irish countryside. A continuity of spirit, a reverence for the life-giving flame intact from when man first struck

two stones together and watched in amazement as flames leaped from the sparks. A living link with the past extinguished forever in our central heating lifetime.

Our family had few options for the morning meal so toast, and sometimes a boiled egg, was the limit of our extravagance.

---

[3] (I rake this fire like everyone else, Brigit below it with Mary on top; twelve angels of the angels of the graces, protecting my house till dawn.)

Having no electricity, toasters weren't an option — but that doesn't mean there was no toast. Not at all! The hot coals were stacked up and a fork inserted in a slice of bread that was then held to the fire. Organic toast you might say! But hot work indeed, so the longer the fork the less discomfort to the toaster!

Winter was the dormant period when, with summer's labour over, only maintenance of farm stock was required. As the lengthening nights stole the daylight hours, the summer-sleek cows, swollen bellies heavy with calf, grazed ever closer to their winter quarters. In the quiet harvest evenings, lit by a slanting sun, they waited patiently at the gate that led towards the byres. Contemplatively chewing interminable cuds they seemed to know instinctively that it would not be long now before the hinges swung open and they would be allowed into the warm shed. Calves bawled impatiently, hungrily, as the grass grew scarce and tasteless.

Once, when one of our cows fell sick a wise neighbour finding no visible signs of illness enquired:

'Is she chewing the cud?'

' No,' my father replied, 'come to think of it, she's not!'

'Well, looks like she's lost it then.'

'Lost it,' my father replied incredulously, 'how could a cow lose the cud? Isn't that just regurgitated hay they're chewing?'

'Well, you can take it from me that they do! You better go right away and find someone has a goat. Goats have two, you can take one for the cow and the goat'll be none the worse. If you like I'll do it for you'

'Right so then, go ahead.'

The cud was duly acquired and the cow quickly regained good health. The goat owner was furious though and berated my father for stealing his goat's cud.

'Ye stole the bloody goat's cud! What did ye do that for? Now me goat is going to die!'

'Ah, take it easy will ye, yer goat is not going to die. Don't ye know they have two cuds. Your goat is going to be alright, and anyway it wasn't me took it.'

'I don't care who took it. It's your cow that has it and if anything happens to my goat who's fault do you think it is?!'

The cow and the goat having both recovered good health, neighbourly relations were restored and peace and harmony prevailed once more.

The cow byres that stood deserted and bare during the summer months took on a new life. Stone floors were scrubbed, sod and wattle roofs brushed, walls whitewashed. Spiders scrambled for cover as the heather 'besom' reached every corner. Its bristles demolished summer homes and tore away the intricate lace of delicate strands that had captured many an unwary fly. Care was taken not to harm the spider. According to legend it once spun its web to hide the persecuted Christ and again in more recent times concealed the entrance to a cave where the patriot Robert Bruce lay in hiding from pursuing English soldiers. It was valued too as an antiseptic and often a fistful of spider web was gathered from the rafters to staunch a bleeding wound.

Care was taken not to interfere with the array of Brigid's

crosses and blessed palm stuck into the roof timbers that protected the herd from sickness and bad luck. The magical elf stones, tucked into the space between thatch and wall, were left undisturbed too. Finding these special stones, lost by the fairies as they moved through the fields, was a rare thing. The ancients, knowing their significance and value, gathered and kept them as a valuable antidote for elfshot cows. Cows became 'elfshot' when mischievous fairies at play about the night-time fields, tossing their fairy stones from one to the other, carelessly struck a cow. Thus struck, the cow would fall and be unable to rise. The elf stones were then brought out and immersed in water brought from a river that formed the junction of three townlands. Thus fortified, and applied with a special ritual, the water had the power to cure the afflicted cow. When Divine intervention and veterinary medicine failed to bring relief, the gods of the old world could be relied upon!

※

Disinfectant was sprinkled on the flagstones and a fresh covering of hay scattered about the 'sink' and floor where the cows were tied. Vertical posts, ropes and chains by which they were tethered were checked and renewed. Outside, a saffron-bright coat of new laid thatch gleamed over whitewashed walls.

With the arrival of the cows to their winter quarters, the byre became communal property. Space was at a premium so two roosts provided perches for the hens all year round. These perches were installed five feet high over a stone lined drain.

The drain ran behind the cows, so droppings from hens and cows were caught in one efficient channel. Hay-lined wooden tea chests along the opposite wall provided comfort for the hens when they laid their eggs or felt broody. The ass too shared this accommodation in her own private corner and trotted there jauntily. The cows didn't like this arrangement at all but a kick from her hind feet deftly planted, quickly settled any objections from them. Opting to avoid trouble they very wisely stayed out of the way of her flailing hooves.

Indoors at last, each one tied to a wooden post in its own place, the cows exhaled heavily, contentedly, in great snorts of steam. Munching armfuls of fresh hay piled under their heads, their hot breath brought warmth and new life to the building. Anyone entering the building got their hopes up and they looked around expectantly in a clanking of halter chains always on the lookout for food. Cows are not ambitious creatures and require little to make them happy. An armful of hay or a bucket of sliced turnips is usually enough. Winter had commenced and these were familiar sounds reassuring the household that all was well as we moved smoothly through the cycles of the seasons, adapting to the demands, submerged in the work.

Finding new lodgers installed in what they regarded as their exclusive property, the hens expressed their disapproval of the new arrangement by kicking up a racket. They stalked in indignant circles at the entrance casting sidelong glances at the cows inside. How dare they! The air shrilled with a cacophony of outraged squawks as they cackled their objections to sharing lodgings with the winter visitors. Led by their strutting leader, the cock, they kept up their noisy protest, until the gathering darkness and fear of predatory foxes forced them into a wary acceptance of the new order. They retreated hesitantly indoors where they kept up their raucous protestations as they hopped uncertainly, one by one, onto the wooden roosts. From here they stared sulkily and distrustfully at the offending cows who looked around at them with expressions of mild curiosity.

Hens are fractious creatures at the best of times and always seem to argue among themselves before settling down for the night. Relative newcomers to Ireland, we are told, it is said their grumbling is caused by the rain and constantly wet feet and whether to leave Ireland altogether and go back to their Scandinavian homeland in the morning. In the end they are silenced by the cock's advice to wait one more day in the hope that the weather will improve!

ꙮ

Milking by this time had been added to my growing list of responsibilities, as it had also to my younger brother who by now was roped in as a helping hand as well. The cows being housed at night meant we didn't have to trek out to the fields anymore thus making it easier to get the day's round of work completed. The fact of their being tied was an additional bonus that meant the bored creature couldn't just walk away when she lost interest in the process or decided she had had enough, as she often did in the field. 'Milking parlours' would come much, much later!

At milking time the glimmer of the cart-lamp candle shed a dim yellow light on the interior of the byre just as it did in Patrick Kavanagh's poem: *A Christmas Childhood*

> *'Outside in the cow-house my mother*
> *Made the noise of milking;*
> *The light of her stable-lamp was a star*
> *And the frost of Bethlehem made it twinkle.'*

Cows munched and nuzzled hay with steamy breaths. The whish-whish of the twin streams of milk that squirted rhythmically into the can as we squeezed the cow's teats: these were comforting sounds. A creamy froth built on top as the vessel resonated from a tinny high pitch at first to a mellow bass as it filled. Milking cows then meant more than just an efficient extraction of product as it does now. The unruly, motorised, mechanical rattle of milking machines, the hurly burly, was a long way off. Commercialisation had not yet stamped out tranquillity.

Sometimes my brother and I squeezed a thin arching white stream towards the waiting cats and laughed as they licked and darted with little pink, open mouths darting like eels to catch the milk that squirted all over their furry faces. At other times we engaged in forbidden milk fights using the cow's teat as a natural water or, in this case, milk pistol. Looking down the years it's not difficult to understand why such irresponsible behaviour must have been a great source of frustration to hard working parents! Parents never learn it seems and have fond and perpetually unrealistic expectations of responsible behaviour from giddy offspring.

One of the hazards of milking was the ever present danger of a sloppy slap on the face from the cow's tail as she flicked it around. Sometimes the misbehaving appendage got wrapped about the milker's head and face. This was unpleasant at any time but particularly disagreeable when it was laden with a thick brown, mucky coating caused by an over-indulgence of lush aftergrass, a natural laxative that was digested and excreted onto the cow's tail. Looking back I believe it was this experience that provoked my first exasperated experimentation with expletives I had heard the older men use!

'**SHIT**', I howled in frustration, and shit indeed it was.

Cows differed very much in temperament. Some were patient, others were not. Some seemed to understand they should remain still during milking, others did not. They regarded the two-legged creatures pulling at their teats as an unfair and unnatural imposition at worst or somewhat of a nuisance at best. Quite often a full can of milk went flying when a nervous cow lashed out with her foot. Or worse still, when she lifted a shitty, hairy hoof and put it down — right in the middle of the can. When this happened it took some explaining to parents whose existence depended on every drop of milk they could send to the creamery!

Before starting to milk we squeezed the first few drops on the ground as an offering to the fairies while saying, 'in the name of the Father, Son and Holy Ghost'. Feeding the fairies while calling on the Holy Trinity may seem a contradiction, but it's a wise man who keeps all sides with him! For those of a fatalistic bent, if the cow kicked and spilled the can of milk, pragmatism kicked in:

'Ah, take it for luck, maybe some poor creature wanted that,' they would say.

Being the oldest my father generally blamed me when things went wrong. Believing the cow to be at fault I felt this was grossly unfair. After all I didn't tell her put her foot in there; there was nothing I could do about two ton of beast deciding to put her foot wherever she liked — but there was no persuading him and the more I protested the angrier he got. Having to take the rap for the cows transgression didn't help my relationship with the beast at all. Very soon the rapport between man and animal needed for a smooth milking operation went from bad to worse. Cows rely on instinct. You can't make a deal with them. Their inherent sense told them I was getting very frustrated at being blamed for their bad behaviour. And they were right. This made them even more nervous and more likely to upset the can, and anyone who thinks that these jobs are all part of pleasant and placid pastoral pursuits — are wrong!

Looking back I don't think I was ever cut out to be a farmer.

Cow's teats differed in size and varied in the ease with which the milk could be drawn. Modern machines eliminate such difficulties but back then it made a difference. Some cows had teats that would fill the milker's fist. With these it was possible to get a good grip and milking was almost always easy. Others had small teats that had to be milked by a stripping motion, using the thumb and two fingers lubricated by dipping the fingers into the milk. Regardless of teat size some farmers could not milk with dry hands although milking wet was condemned as unhygienic by dairy inspectors. Then there were cows that could hold on to their milk, especially if they looked around, which they almost always did, and didn't like who was doing the milking. They had their favourites too! Some, women milkers especially, sang while they were milking. It had the effect of soothing them allowing the milk to flow more easily. On bigger farms, where help could be afforded, farms girls employed for work in the dairy with good voices got better wages than those that could not sing!

But don't take my word for it! English visitor Fynes Moryson writing in the 1600s came across headstrong cows: 'The Irish cowes are so stubborne', he wrote, that , 'as many tymes they will not be milked but by some one woman, when, how, and by whom they list. If their calves be taken from them, or they otherwise grew stubborn, the skins of the Calves stuffed with straw must be set by them to smell on, and many fooleries done to please them, or else they will yield no milk.'

Equally unimpressed by the rebellious Irish he observed that the, 'inhabitants of that time were no less compliant in their obedience to the State, than their beasts were to them'.

Regarding other denizens of the farmyard turkeys come to mind. The onset of shorter days brought changes for the thirty or so turkeys we reared for the Christmas market. They were rounded up and housed earlier now. Weighing twenty pounds or more these were large birds that required a lot of space, so they had their own dedicated quarters.

Industrious foragers, they scavenged meadow and stubble methodically during the day. They were the show-offs of the farmyard. On fine evenings, craws stuffed, and puffed up with turkey importance, the cocks strutted about importantly in proud and ostentatious displays. Guldering loudly, wings stretched to the ground like Spanish galleons at full sail, they took off in short, quick bursts of speed across the cobblestones. Red necks ablaze in fiery splendour they made a fine spectacle. Unimpressed, the turkey hens looked on. Maintaining their dignity, they took no part in these intemperate exhibitions. 'Boys will be boys' they seemed to be thinking as they looked on indulgently.

Added to my growing list of responsibilities was the rounding up of this rowdy flock and housing them for the night. My chief interest in the evenings at that time was to get the chores out of the way fast so I could go off 'rambling' to a neighbour's house for card-playing or conversation. Unmoved by these turkey-world displays I hurried them with undignified haste to their night quarters. Sometimes their wild, tree-bred, turkey instincts rebelled at any kind of confinement. They were the bane of my young life as, on fine evenings, some notion of a formerly wild and free existence awakening in them, they made defiant bids for freedom and staged periodic turkey rebellions. Showing no deference to my authority, or for my plans for the evening, first one bird, then another, and then the whole flock took to the air with a wild graceless flapping.

All I could do was watch helplessly while they circled around to land on the highest point of the outbuildings. Safely out of reach, the turkey rebels perched aloft. Red necks stretched and swivelling about, they looked down at me defiantly as if they were thinking in their turkey minds, 'What are ye going to do about that?'

Carried away by the impulse, they couldn't have given any thought to the inevitable consequences of such subversive behaviour. With gay abandon they risked all for a wild instant of illusory freedom. Living for the moment nothing was learned from previous ill-considered experimentations at resisting the inevitable — and I didn't have time to waste on pondering the workings of turkey minds.

Luckily for the mutinous birds my mother was around most of the time to protect them. When she wasn't I pegged clods of turf to knock them down. Well-aimed shots dislodged them from their lofty perches without injuring anything but their pride. A good shot and a direct hit forced an undignified submission and an unsteady return to earth.

My mother had a sixth sense for this sort of thing. She had an intuitive perception of the danger to her charges. No matter where she was she invariably rushed on to the scene shortly after hostilities commenced. Her irate: 'What in God's name are y'at there!?' meant other ways had to be found to bring the birds down. Persisting in my method of turkey control only meant that hostilities would open on another front and this time I would be at the receiving end. At times like this, where my mother was concerned, and it came to a choice between me and the turkeys, I knew I didn't have a chance! They were an important source of income to her so no irresponsible or cavalier treatment of such a vital asset would be tolerated. As well as that she had a real fondness for them. Having coaxed, nurtured and fed them through sickness and health from the day they were hatched they were like children to her. She was strange like that. She became genuinely attached to cows, calves and turkeys; yet her affection didn't extend to any prolonged grieving when the calves went to the butcher or the turkeys to the Christmas table.

When she was around, gentler, albeit slower methods of persuasion had to be found. Coaxed and threatened by turns, they were eventually talked down and shooed into their house. Here they showed no inclination at all for high places; when they were wanted to fly, they didn't. Subdued but still contrary, they had to be lifted up onto their roosts, poles that stretched from wall to wall at about three feet from the ground. I wouldn't care where they spent the night but allowing them to indulge their preference for lying on the ground caused deformed breast bones, according to my mother, and a consequent lower price at market.

When Christmas was over all that remained of our turkey band was one lone female to provide the basis of next year's flock. Unaware of her great good fortune, she wandered disconsolately about, grieving the companions of her one glorious, carefree summer. Bewildered by the speedy turn of events, it was beyond her ken to know what had brought about such a speedy change of fortune. The yard seemed too quiet now without her family's noisy, strutting performances and in her turkey way she seemed to grieve for them. She never had to socialise with the hens before. They spoke a strange language she did not understand. Now, her despairing attempts to ingratiate herself with them met with no success and they made great dashes at her. Clucking agitatedly they chased her, driving her away with their sharp beaks.

A week or so before Christmas this lone survivor's family had been gathered together and shipped off to the annual market. Rounded up in the early morning, legs tied tightly together, they were suspended one by one, upside down, from the hook of the scales. My father held them up while my mother, peering with a great intensity at the figures on the brass face of the dial, carefully noted and marked down the weight of each one. A lot of hard work had gone into bringing them this far and she was going to make sure there would be no short weight given by some shady dealer in Kinlough where the market was held. Prices in the late '50's ranged from 1s/10d to 2s per lb.for the smaller and lighter hens to 1s/6d and 1s/8d for cocks that could weigh up to twenty five pounds. Breast bones were checked too. A crooked breast meant an even lower price from the buyer.

As each turkey was probed, tied and weighed, it was deposited in the ass cart that had been fitted with a slatted 'crib'. I couldn't help feeling sorry for them now. Tightly packed together, they huddled on the floor of the cart like condemned prisoners in some medieval setting. But I was glad too; my sympathy was tempered with the comforting thought that now I didn't have to look after them anymore. In addition, there would be money and resulting good humour in the house when they were sold. And sold they would be as there was always demand for what would much later be known as 'free-range' turkeys.

It was an important day for the shopkeepers too. A good market meant they could count on something getting paid off the book. Good or bad, they were sure to get something. There were no regular paydays for farmers and therefore no money to pay for the daily or weekly shopping. An account book was kept and it was expected that when produce was sold a portion would be paid on the account. There was no fixed figure; people paid what they could afford and it was very rarely that the balance could be cleared completely.

The cart moved out of the farm yard and jolted on to the rough, stone paved country road. It was joined by others similarly laden and soon a long line of the brightly coloured orange vehicles rattled in procession to the market town. All semblance of dignity gone, the bewildered creatures, heads extended from the slatted sides of the cart, vanished gradually from view as vehicle and cargo disappeared over the brow of the hill. Seeming to sense it was all over, was it my imagination, or did they look back at me through the slats of the cart with reproachful eyes. Despite our occasional differences they had looked on me as a friend. After all hadn't I spent long hours plucking the wholesome bags of nettles and comfrey that, boiled, reared them from when they were chicks? I had to turn my head away as their mournful faces reproved my betrayal. I was not their friend after all.

The close contact that came from rearing turkeys created an emotional bond that wrenched the hearts of owners, some more than others. The bustle of activity and gravity of the preparations on this day were always lightened by a tender-hearted neighbour who made no attempt to conceal his grief. Tears rolled down his cheeks as he watched them bump on down the rough road on the iron shod ass cart. We thought this very funny and laughed ourselves silly as he waved after the turkeys and they looked back disconsolately at him, their long red necks sticking out of the side of the cart swaying gracefully to the motion of the vehicle.

Late in the 1950's an enterprising neighbour who owned a small van, seeing a business opportunity, let it be known that he would be available for the transportation of the turkeys. His offer was accepted and a carnival atmosphere lent to the occasion that year as he ferried back and forth all day long with cargos of doomed gobblers. It was turning out to be a very successful venture so, in celebration of this, each trip to Kinlough was punctuated by a visit to the pub.

A man of high good humour at any time, his spirit and wit grew with each trip. Feathers flew, turkeys guldered, people laughed and Patrick cheered as the luckless creatures were motored to their fate. It was, 'as good as a circus', everyone agreed afterwards and the technological leap in that year from humble ass to high class van is still fondly remembered!

Even though we raised fat turkeys to sell at the Christmas market no steaming, drumsticks in the air, well-basted gobbler, graced our holiday table. We reared them but we couldn't afford to eat one. Having looked after them all year they were nothing special to us anyway. Fat duck, goose or hen pleased us just as well. It was a meal fit for a lord, and we called no man Master on that day:

> *'Our kitchen floor of pot-hole clay*
> *Was changed as we read,*
> *To a carpeted room on Christmas Day.*
> *Romance was in every head.*
> *A brandy-flamed pudding came in on a tray*
> *Carried high by a well off Dad'* [4]

Winter deepened and the slings and arrows of outrageous winter advanced inexorably in earth's unending cycle. It was hard to endure its perpetual gales, it's piling snow, frozen ground and biting frost. Thus was spent the winter slicing turnips, feeding hay, maintaining livestock, staying alive, keeping warm, marking time.

When the storms blew hard off the Atlantic men were on the move at first light to be the first to grab whatever opportunistic treasure might have been driven ashore. Bales of rubber were worth a small fortune when sold to local merchants. Logs and planks were used to make carts, wheelbarrows, ladders and gates. The occasional barrel of whiskey was celebrated. It was all an underground industry as Gardai and Revenue officials were diligent in the pursuit of 'State property'. These arms of the law were regarded with dread.

[4] *The Old Time Christmas Story*, Patrick Kavanagh

They slept warmly in their beds while these hunter-gathers risked death, drew their treasure home and hid it from prying eyes. Their law was the natural law. Items recovered from the sea logically belonged to the men who risked their lives to collect it. It made sense. Anything else was bad law. But law, good or bad, was law and the statute books stated clearly that anything recovered from the sea was the property of the State.

Christmas was as welcome a respite for us as Saturnalia was for the ancient Romans. The festival of the Christ Child was wonderful to contemplate, but a visit from the Mummers was another highlight of the holiday.

'It wouldn't be the same without them!' everyone agreed.

Their visit was announced by a rough knocking on the door: 'Any room for Mummers'?'

The invitation accepted, the door burst open and a strange looking masked figure dressed in rags, decorated with ribbons and papers leaped with a few mad bounds into the kitchen. A draught of air whirling through the open door sent the flame of the oil lamp dancing wildly. The disturbed light sent grotesque shadows pirouetting along the whitewashed wall from the maniacal figure in the middle of the floor. I ran terrified from the table to hide behind my father in the corner and watched as the menacing character, like some mad hobgoblin of the dark, turning in sharp and crazy circles, paced across the flagstones shouting and gesturing. Following him a motley array of creatures with strange names: Captain, Green Knight, Oliver Cromwell, Beelzebub and Devil Doubt paraded in quick succession each one reciting a strange gibberish of words.

I watched wide-eyed as over in the corner a fight broke out between Prince George and St. Patrick. After a fierce struggle with swords and clubs Prince George dropped mortally wounded to the floor. A mad doctor strode in immediately with an array of potions professing to cure the fallen man with:

*'the foo of the fee the hillis the bee, nine pills, nine tills, nine fortnights before day, and if that doesn't cure I'll ask no pay. Rise up dead man and fight again'*

Miraculously the dead man rose from the floor upon which the Captain called on different members of the party in turn to dance, sing or play an instrument. The strange company played and danced around the floor taking the fireside ramblers out with them.

The performance over, the Mummers skipped out into the darkness. As the sounds of the accordion and *bodhran* faded away in the distance these phantoms of the night carried my imagination with them.

It was only in later years we would understand the deeper significance of this seemingly nonsensical play. With the days getting shorter and shorter approaching the winter solstice our ancestors believed that the waning sun was in imminent danger of disappearing altogether. Something must be done to please the gods and encourage the light and longer days to return. The result of their deliberations at Newgrange was the life-giving symbolism represented by the sun as a male agent entering and impregnating the womb-like structure of the passage grave. The beam, representing life itself, released the spirits of the dead into a new existence. From that moment the light revived and the days grow longer.

From time immemorial the Christmas Mummers have practised sympathetic magic to achieve the same result. Of the two figures that fight, one represents the Light and the other the Dark. The dark figure falls symbolising the death of the old year. Dr Brown's magical incantations can achieve any consequence he desires simply by simulating the problem, treating it, and transferring the desired result by a process of cause and effect to the affected body: in this case nothing less than the movement of the sun and planets.

Day followed day, the pleasant hiatus of the Christmas holiday passed, and the winter months ground relentlessly on.

'Nothing lasts forever' my mother said cheerfully as she stripped Christmas decorations from wall, dresser and window. Nothing ever seemed to bother that woman:

'Ye can see a stretch in th'evenings already. Every day getting' longer now by a cock's step in the duncle,' she declared happily!

And so it was. Shortly now would come the Spring when life's cycle renews, hens and the solitary turkey would grow broody and a new crop of calves arrive from the heavily pregnant cows. The golden promise of a new year, new beginnings — all things are possible and hope springs again.

*'We sleep and wake and sleep,*
*but all things move;*
*The Sun flies forward to his*
*brother Sun;*

*The dark Earth follows,*
*Wheel'd in her ellipse, and*
*human things return upon themselves,*
*Thro' all the circle of the*
*golden year.'* [5]

With the arrival of Spring and calving time there were days of anxious waiting and watching. Profound observations were made by my father and visiting neighbours. How advanced was the lactation or 'springing'? Was she 'soft' meaning was the vulva swollen enough to indicate imminent birth? Particularly coming on nightfall the final arbiter was the pelvic or 'calf bones'. Were they up or down? The advice of trusted neighbours, experts on these matters, was sought. Having carefully studied the expectant animal judgement was pronounced on whether the calf was likely to arrive that night or perhaps 'she might last it out till morning' in which case it was safe to go to bed. Sometimes it was difficult to tell because the bones, like the grand old Duke of York, would be neither up nor down. When that happened my father paced restlessly. 'You're in and out there like a clockin' hen,' my mother would declare laughing.

After much deliberating it was decided on one particular evening that Bluebell's bones, for that was the cows name, were sufficiently depressed to indicate that the birth couldn't be far off. It might happen during the night.

'Well,' my father said, announcing the decision to my mother

5  The Golden Year, Alfred Lord Tennyson

who was fussing about the kitchen making the evening meal, 'looks like there'll be no sleep tonight!'

'Oh well, what about it,' she replied, 'sure if there's a healthy calf in the morning it'll all be worthwhile. Sit down and have a bite to eat, I'm after making pratie bread, don't worry about it.'

'Pratie' or potato bread was my father's favourite as it was, and still is, along with boxty, mine. The pungent fragrance of turf smoke pervaded the kitchen. A cheery light and bright flames from the fire warmed it. Bubbling contentedly on the hob the soot blackened cast iron kettle gave a soothing musical backdrop, comforting sounds in the way of always that told us everything was well with our world.

On one sidewall a ruby light glimmered from the blood-red globe of the Sacred Heart lamp, a constant vigil before the mournful face of Christ. Exposed heart banded with barbwire, he gazed perpetually skywards seeming to implore favours from a heavenly father for our sinful humanity. Holy water glistened in a font hung near the front door; a talisman that safeguarded us from the devil and from lightning; sprinkles from its bowl protected and brought luck on trips away from home by day or night, to fair or field.

At the other end of the room the delph-lined dresser, its mugs and bowls arranged immaculately, was a modest showpiece. A wooden moulding across the top concealed my father's small store of tools: builders level, bicycle pump, pincers, hoof-parer for the ass and such. Tucked safely inside a storage space at the bottom were dusty treasures of his seafaring days: charts, dividers, parallel rule, compass. These strange objects I often pulled out and examined with a child's curious eyes but the questions I put to my father were answered only with a brusque:

'Put that back where ya got it.'

It was my mother that told me what these items were and how precious they were to him. Perhaps now that he was chained to the family farm, he didn't want to be reminded of his younger seafaring days and the untrammelled freedom of the ocean where his heart really belonged. While he couldn't part with those objects that were once such an important part of his life he preferred that they remained, like his memories, cocooned and concealed.

The kitchen table alongside the other wall, draped with a knife-scored oil-cloth worn through from use, was built of sturdy pine, one of the homemade items constructed long ago, as was the cradle of my infancy, from *eadaills* — planks of wood and other flotsam — pushed in by the fierce storms and gathered perilously along the shore at *Ros na Rí* and other tide swept inlets. The covering, its once bright flower printed pattern cracked and faded, concealed the scars of antiquity marking the planks and sturdy, scrubbed legs of the timbers underneath.

Once when the oilcloth needed replacing my father thought he would economise and dispense with it altogether. His inner artist blossoming he painted the table white. Next he cut a flower pattern on an old cork fishing float from under the dresser. Rummaging about in the shed he found a discarded tin of crusted green paint in which he dipped the cork. Dabbing artfully at the white background he soon transformed the stolid wood into a handsome enough imitation of a flowered tablecloth.

The family cat had been observing all of this activity with sleepy eyes from its usual place beside the fire. Deciding suddenly to investigate it jumped up on the table from where she was quickly ejected with a fierce **SCAT!** and a swipe of a wet dishcloth from my mother. But not quick enough, as a trail of pawmarks now ran across the newly painted table. A smudged pattern at the end marked the spot where my mother had put an abrupt end to the cats exploring.

'Bloody cat! Get out to hell outa that ye useless thing,' she shouted, hunting the now chastened would be ratter out the door with great swipes of the sweeping brush.

'And what are you laughing at?,' she exclaimed looking around angrily at my father who saw the funny side of it and didn't mind the artistic addition to his masterpiece at all.

'You and your bright ideas,' she yelled, 'Will ye look at the table and the mess of it, you have no more sense than the cat.'

꿏

In the evenings, the day's worries and work done we sat around the kitchen table chatting about the events of the day. Above, a paraffin lamp hung from a nail driven into the lime-crusted wall. It's yellow eye lit the little family group gathered there: father, mother my younger brother and I. The glow from its hairpin-straddled globe illuminated dimly the ancient walls, religious pictures, the white-scrubbed flagstone floor. Embracing the burnished, oak beamed sod roof overhead the pale light was lost in shadowy gloom above the smoke blackened rafters. Stone walls, heavy with a thousand coats of whitewash and veined with a network of cracks, disclosed centuries of existence. As I remember the scene on this March morning our kitchen had the character and warm ambience of an old oil painting.

'Spare the butther!' my mother cried as we lashed it on to the pratie bread. Even though we supplied the milk that made the butter it was one of the more expensive items on the shopping list, its value having increased on its way from cow to creamery to churn, packaging and then to wholesaler before it landed on the retailer's shelf.

The discussion on this particular February evening centred around the task in hand for the night.

'Well you're getting on in years now, and you have a day's planting to do tomorrow, maybe time for someone else to take on this job?,' my mother said, addressing my father. 'It's not that it's hard work.
What about you Joe? D'ye think you'd be fit for it?'

I hadn't a care in the world up to that as these matters were always taken care of by adults. Although moving in a parallel world their concerns were somehow remote from mine. The unexpected offer took me by surprise. This was a man's job and it was always my father who kept vigil. The prospect of added responsibility was intimidating, and yet proud to have been asked I agreed — which was just as well because a refusal would have been met with only with annoyance at best, or a lash or two of the sally rod at worst. Such an advance on my involuntary career was in actuality an ultimatum or at least an offer that couldn't be refused. Growing up on a farm it wasn't like you really had a choice as you might have had had your father been a carpenter or a plumber or some other trade or profession. And so it was that bit by bit I was drawn gradually and inevitably into a fuller participation in the daily routine.

My mother wasn't finished at that. There was no stopping her once she got going:

'And ye know what else I'm thinking,' she added. 'wouldn't it be a good thing to give Joe a bit more responsibility, and a bit of independence as well. Suppose we give him a cow...'

'Give him a cow! What do you mean give him a cow! Where are we going to get...'

'Ahh stop. Would ye listen to me for a minute! What I'm thinking is when this cow calves he can look after her, we'll have the milk of course but he can take the responsibility of looking after Bluebell and then getting next year's calf. He can raise the calf, sell it when it's a stirk and in that way have some money for himself with enough left over to buy another younger calf. In that way bit by bit he can build a herd of his own —and we'll still have the cow.'

Her logic was irrefutable!

'I don't know, where is the extra land going to come from to feed more cattle, we have hardly enough as it is?'

'Look Petie, we have to start somewhere, give the lad an interest, something of his own. If it doesn't work out, it doesn't, but nothing ventured, nothing gained!'

That was my mother all over, always looking for ways to improve, 'That fella has no push in him,' she'd declare while busying herself looking for ways to raise another calf, have a few more hens or turkeys for the Christmas market. In fairness it must be said that my father, having served as a Volunteer during the War of Independence, and endured a hunger strike during the Civil War, had delicate health. Years on the run sleeping in rough shelters on hillsides in damp clothes had taken their toll.

This new departure, the sudden opportunity for promotion, was a lot to take in. Could I measure up to the challenge? Would I be strong enough? Was I ready to cross this threshold into a man's world? I could feel the safety net of childhood dropping away. Like most young people desiring freedom I didn't want the responsibility, and this seemed like a whole lot of that. The thought of owning my own cow —a placid Shorthorn cross with blue colouration, hence the name Bluebell — even if it was more like a lease, tipped the balance. I was finally going to be somebody, not just a shadow of my parents.

Prancing about all night cows on the verge of giving birth became more and more restless. No sooner would they lie down than they were up again. Up and down, up and down. This could go on for hours until finally they lay on their side pressing and bawling in the pangs of calf birth. Then the water bag emerged and the calf's feet could be seen moving on the inside. When the water broke, or was punctured manually, much strenuous pulling, sometimes with a rope attached to the feet, was needed as the head and forelegs were coaxed and encouraged into the world. Eventually the calf slid out on to the floor in a rush of amniotic fluid, calf bed and membrane.

I knew that's how it went from subsequent experience. This time on my first watch I had fallen asleep by the fire. Waking with a start I rushed out and there was the newborn calf slithering about in the muck on the floor. What an inauspicious beginning to my new life. Panic set in: I'm in big trouble! What's my parents, who put so much trust in me, going to say? I can't cover up, too late for that. What am I going to do?! I had to act quick; the calf could be lost. Rushing into the house, I roused my father and told him about the birth, glossing over the fact that I wasn't there when it happened. Thankfully he didn't ask and just muttered a gruff, sleepy: 'Why didn't ye call me?' We carried it then, upside down with its dangly head tucked between extremely slippery forelegs, from the byre to the kitchen and placed it on a bed of hay.

My mother was out of bed now too and danced attendance on the cow who looked around at all the fuss, missing her calf no doubt as well, with big wild eyes. Now that I look back on it my mother probably understood the procedure a lot better than the men, understood from experience the agony of birth. She mixed a poultice of oatmeal and placed it in the hollows near the 'calf bones' on the cow's back and fed the exhausted creature a mixture of bran and sliced turnips. The calf she fed with the 'beestings' or colostrum, the first milk of the cow. She made a delicious curd from the leftover milk that was a big treat for everyone: the first fruit of spring.

Satisfaction showed on my father's face as he rubbed down

the struggling, spindly animal thoroughly with fistfuls of hay. The calf was tied with a length of rope to an iron peg in the floor and a 'ponger' or tin muzzle, with holes punched in it for breathing, secured over his snout to prevent it from choking on wisps of hay. Here it would stay for a week or two until it became strong and healthy on which it was placed in the byre with the other cattle. This new arrival might have been the pride of the family and its arrival securing our welfare — particularly if it was a more valuable black bull calf — but the strongest memory I have is of breakfasts ruined by the smell emanating from the friendly calf as he stared curiously at us while performing his bodily functions. My mother was, as always, pragmatic: 'Shittin' luck is the best of luck,' she said, quoting an old proverb.

Older now and full of promise I looked with some satisfaction at the new arrival, secure in the knowledge that my failure hadn't been found out and thought smugly: 'it might take a while but next year that calf is going to be mine...'

The lifestyle and practices described here might today seem a mark of want, but the opposite is true; everything is relative and not everyone then had enough land to keep cows. For those who kept pigs it was not unusual to see sows, when they were ready to farrow, brought into the kitchen and placed on a bed of straw. They were kept there for a week or so until the piglets became strong. The 'pig in the parlour' was a sign of prosperity, not poverty. In a pre-mechanised age it is how successful small farms were run, and had been for many centuries. A bucketful of water, strong washing soda and diligent application of a strong scrubbing brush left the kitchen flagstones gleaming white as before.

With this new birth Spring was announced. Nature had awakened and as it progressed into summer it was not only 'young men's fancy' that turned to love. The animals too were eyeing each other up with that instinctive urge for procreation. Hens stopped laying and went 'clocking' (broody). It was time then to put down a 'setting' of eggs, preferably from a neighbouring village so as to prevent inbreeding. Any more than one or two 'clockers' was very unwelcome as only a small number of settings were required to replenish the flock. Surplus hens that got ideas of getting into the family business surplus to the farm's requirements were quickly disabused of the notion. They were put under a creel or pannier and doused occasionally with buckets of cold water 'to take the clocking off them' and encourage them back in the business of laying their valuable eggs.

The lone turkey that had survived the Christmas slaughter also started to 'crouch', meaning she too went broody and went about the yard doing exactly that: crouching in a submissive posture to receive the turkey cock. Only there was no mate for her! While the hens had the farmyard cock for a paramour, the unfortunate turkey had no such luck. She had to be conveyed to a breeding turkey cock, a suitor that lived many miles away —and this set of circumstances led to the most embarrassing experience of many a young person's life.

'Would ye take that turkey up to Kilfeather's?' my mother said. WithouthavingitspelledoutIimmediatelyknewwhatthatmeant.

'Kilfeathers? What about Kennedy's in Ballinagaddy, it's closer.'

'No, take her to Kilfeather's!'

My face was turning red already just thinking about the prospect. The shorter trip would have saved me a lot of embarrassment! The reason for her choice of stud may have been linked to Kilfeather's having a State registered pedigree cock. It may also have helped that we were distantly related to them. Either way once my mother made up her mind there was no changing it:

'C'mon here, get the bike, I'll catch her.'

There was no getting out of it. So we chased the bird around the yard and catching it, tied its legs together and placed it in an old shopping bag. This was hung on the handlebars of the bike and off I reluctantly went down the road. The turkey's long neck waved out of the bag and it must have been a draw as to whose face was redder: the turkey's or mine. Faced with the prospect of meeting any of the boys and girls I knew, and the consequent laughing and mocking —'Hey would ye look at Mc Gowan with the turkey!' — I ran the gauntlet and pedalled as furiously as I could.

'Hey Mc Gowan, ya big eejit, are ye on a date, haw, haw, haw?'

It was the school bully and there could be no taking of prisoners. I had to show him how tough I really was.

'Ah, would ye ever fuck off with yerself ya silly oul' bollocks!'

'Get down off that bike and I'll show ye who's the bollocks.'

'Ah I wouldn't bother me arse with ye ya big cissy!'

It was all bluff though and I was mortified as I knew the news of Mc Gowan and the turkey was going to be all over the grapevine. Beating a hasty retreat I broke all land speed records for a bicycle between Killawaddy and Kiltykere. Mrs Kilfeather introducing my turkey to hers ushered me into the kitchen to a snack of lemonade and sweet cake.

'You stay there now *agradh*,' she said, 'I'll be back in a minute. I want to see how these two birds are getting on.'

A chatty, friendly woman she shortly came back into the kitchen and: 'Take your time there now sonny and you can head away home whenever you're ready. How's all the family at home? Tell your father and mother I must go down and see them sometime soon.'

We chatted a while, half a crown changed hands, the price of the turkey's service, and I headed away for home hoping no one would see me on the return journey.

'Was there any turkeys there before you?' My mother asked on my arrival which I thought was a strange question. What difference did it make whether there was or not!

'Naw, there wasn't.'

I was very glad when the courtship was over and our turkey finally settled down to hatch the eggs that must have been very well fertilised by Mrs Kilfeathers amorous turkey cock.

All of this was fine, but when was my ship going to come in? The days were long in waiting for Bluebell's connubial instincts to kick in. A February or March calf was ideal so given that a cow's gestation period was nine months, the same as that for a person, she would have to come 'round', (in heat) in May or June.

The weeks went by and gradually more calves arrived and new chicks emerged from the hen and turkey eggs so carefully tended by mother. Soon the mother hen introduced her brood to the kitchen floor. Bright-eyed, red combs at a jaunty angle, heads angled expectantly, when they ventured in they were welcome visitors. My father didn't like the mess and shooed them out:

'Bloody hens', he'd yell.

But he knew where his crust came from and tolerated it when my mother threw a fistful of 'Injun' meal on the floor for them to eat. They ate it hungrily and as gratefully as a hen can be, left their calling card, and departed as they had come. No harm was done. There were no carpets. Once again lashings of hot water and a sturdy scrubbing brush washed away dirt and calling cards and left the flagstones clean and bright. If the pig was 'the gentleman that paid the rent' then the hen was surely the lady that bought the groceries.

The fireside became a haven, a recovery ward, for the sickly chicks and turkeys that took the 'pip'. Choking and gasping like asthmatic drunks on the worms that clogged their windpipes it seemed there was no hope for them. But this resourceful woman knew exactly what to do. Taking them in a firm grip on her lap she held their beaks, one by one, and gently pulled their tongue out to reveal the windpipe. Braiding a horsehair into a mini plait she pushed and eased it expertly down. When she withdrew it, trapped in the weave of the horsehair were the squirming white maggots that caused the debility. She nursed the chick, the heat restored them and her patients almost always recovered.

Spring moved on, cows were let out to distant pastures, crops were sown: potatoes, turnips, mangels, grain — and May a long time in coming. Bluebell grew sleek with spring grass and produced cans of milk to overflowing; her calf became a strong healthy animal. Coming into May I kept a close eye on her but was not sure exactly what to look out for. Day after day she grazed impassively swiping her tail at the flies that annoyed her, chewing the cud when she was full.

Sex, whether it be animals or people, in 1950's Ireland was a four letter word and not discussed. Even where animals were concerned it's manifestations were learned by observation and a kind of osmosis. Sex between people was an unfathomable mystery learned from schoolmates who bluffed a lot, exaggerated the little bit they knew and made up the rest of it. Rude doggerels gave no insight:

"Long and thin goes too far in and doesn't suit the ladies
It's short and thick that does the trick
And manufactures babies."

Some of us, maybe even most of us, hadn't the foggiest notion what that was all about but nodded knowledgeably anyway and laughed with the old-fashioned boys, disguising our ignorance as best we could. Pretences like this were vital if we were to hold our tenuous place in the all-important hierarchy of peers. It didn't seem so at the time but in retrospect it seems that those who laughed the loudest knew the least.

City dwellers believed that country children had an advantage, that they were introduced to sex in a natural way, that it happened as a normal interaction in their daily environment. We didn't see it like that at all! The cock did it with the hens out in the 'dunkle'. The dogs in the street did it with gusto. The ram engaged the sheep with frenetic enthusiasm. The bull did it with the cow in the field. But they were only animals. Neither inspiration or education was acquired by such observation. You wouldn't be surprised what the lower orders might get up to. Cows ate grass in the field. Humans didn't. Somehow we didn't apply animal behaviour to anything that people might do. Some degree of decorum was expected from them.

Late in May a sudden change came over Bluebell. Normally a quiet beast she became restless, wandering wildly around the pasture fields, bawling loudly. It was quite out of character for her and a worrying development. Was my investment in pain? Was she sick? I told my father in case the vet was needed.

'Right!,' he said, 'C'mon we'll go out and have a look at her.'

When we got out to the pasture field all of the cows were restless and excited. Bluebell was mounting the other cows and they in turn rising on her. Even the bullocks, castrated males, were getting in on the act, going through the motions. Unperturbed by her erratic behaviour my father walked around studying her carefully. A clear discharge came from her hind quarter and her tail was held to one side.

'She's 'round' (in heat) for sure,' he finally concluded, 'but you'll be time enough to take her to the bull till morning. We'll put her into the byre.'

Good news at last then. My ship had come in — or at least the keel was about to be laid! I didn't mind taking the cow to the bull as somehow it wasn't as ridiculous a sight as taking the turkey to the cock. It seemed more like a man's job.

Bluebell stamped and bawled all night. Her companions out in the field answered sympathetically. Full of manly pride I put a halter with a long lead on her head and set out early in the morning on our four mile trek to the bull. By his glance I could tell my father didn't like a halter being used; he never did. Although never quite saying it he seemingly thought there was something cissyish about using a halter; that the cow should be driven. Certainly it took more skill to drive the animal when it had no restraint.

It was the same on taking cattle to the fair. When black cattle were brought it seemed reasonable to mark the animal in some way. This was done with a bit of coloured thread tied to the tail. There were so many black cattle it was difficult to tell the difference between them. My father discouraged this. I think he felt a good herdsman should be able to tell one from another without such childish aids. It seemed then that everything that was done by the old people had to be done the hard way. There was no easy way for them! And it looked as if they liked it that way. If they found an easy way they'd think there was something wrong with it.

'Don't loop that rope around your hand,' he said sternly, 'If the cow takes off down the road you could be dragged. And whatever you do if there's any strange bulls on the road don't let them near her. Bring her straight to Kennedys. D'ye hear me!'

With those stern warnings ringing in my ears I headed off down the road, and when I was out of sight wrapped the rope securely around my wrist. My investment bank wasn't going to get away and neither was any undeserving bull going to get near her. My calf was going be the perfect one, a pure-bred.

Cattle usually were reluctant to go anywhere they were wanted to go and had to be driven. Unless there was a prize such as a handful of meal or a bucket of turnips at the end they sought every means of escape. Bluebell was no exception — but this time it was different and she set out at a brisk pace. It would be her third calf and her third annual trip to the bull. It seemed like she knew exactly what she wanted, where it was and was keen to get there.

Off we went down the hill, out by the gatehouse, right turn at Cassidy's and then a straight run on the Burra Road to Ballinagaddy. The woods on our right, some scrub pasture with a stand of alders on the left, Ballinagaddy in the distance and Benbulben mountain towering majestically over all. The spicy smell of whin and whitethorn filled the air. Everything was going according to plan and I was quite pleased with myself as we moved smartly along the road.

Then I heard it, a low bellow, half moan, and Bluebell stopped dead in her tracks. I tightened my grip on the rope, and on the strong ash plant I held in the other hand. Like a bulldozer it came out of the bushes. The bull was a massive red brute with sharp pointed horns and a white stripe running from his face down his front legs. A Hereford. He advanced slowly towards us froth slobbering from his mouth, his nose wrinkled up in a frightening grimace. Bluebell almost tore my arm from its socket as she darted towards the newcomer. Had she no shame! I held on with grim determination. Not alone did I not want this match to take place because there would be big trouble when I got home but I also wanted Kennedy's pedigree Aberdeen Angus to be the father of my calf.

The bull continued to advance towards us in a kind of confident certainty that he was the centre of Bluebells attention and their union inevitable. My presence didn't matter. My last uncertain hope was that the wire boundary fence that ran all along the road would stop him. Not a chance! Like a four legged panzer he just rolled over it as if it wasn't there. Slapping her with my ash plant brought no result. She had eyes and feelings only for the intruder. I pushed her: 'Geddap outa that!' urgently, but I might as well have tried to move Benbulben

Bloody cow! I was trying to save her virtue but the brazen hussy didn't care. Trembling, she looked frightened and interested all at the same time. His red eyes, slobbering breath and fierce horns got closer and closer and there was nothing I could do about it. Nothing! If I tackled him directly he outweighed me by at least half a ton. This was a nightmare scenario where many farmers get killed each year by bulls with only one thing on their mind. He moved in, they nuzzled each other, sounding each other out, a kind of introduction almost. Satisfied with what he smelled and saw, and overcome with passion he suddenly wheeled around behind and rose on her. Bluebell didn't move.

I lathered him with my stick. It was no good, he was impervious to pain. In desperation I turned it around in my hand so to hit him with the knob end. I targeted his ears and his snout being the most sensitive places where he would feel pain. Raining blow after desperate blow he still hung doggedly on rising in starts and fits on her. I continued to batter him till the strength left my arms and he slid down off her. Stunned now, and eyes glazed his head fell to the ground. His long penis, stiff before, hung limp and useless now its mission aborted. I turned the stick on my beloved Bluebell and at last she moved reluctantly on.

It was over and I followed with shaken confidence and even more shaky legs.

Going up Kennedy's lane we met a neighbour coming down. Exchanging greetings we passed easily, his cow having accomplished her mission and mine eager to realise hers. Arriving at Kennedy's I explained what had happened. Henry was sympathetic and interested:

'Did he serve her?'

'What?'

'The cow! Did he get it into her?',

Well, I didn't think so but I couldn't be sure as I was too occupied at the other end.

'I don't think so.'

'You don't think so!,' he responded with a hint of a smile. 'Weren't you there'

'No! He didn't. I beat him back before he could,' I ventured with some certainty.

'Right so, he probably didn't. Good man. Stand back there, we'll let this fellow out till we see what happens.'

Led by a ring through his nose the massive Aberdeen Angus was released. The two circled around in a slow courtship dance. The bull rested its head on Bluebell's rump, sniffed at her genitalia, pawed the ground and curled his upper lip to savour the scent. He sniffed, curled and pawed until Bluebell, becoming impatient, turned around and rose on the bull. I suppose that might have been funny but I didn't think so then and neither did Henry:

'Get down outta that,' he said giving her a whack of his ash plant.

The bull was interested but, surprisingly, in no hurry to perform. Henry gave a peculiar kind of high pitched whistle which was probably meant to excite the bull. He whistled, round and round they went and suddenly up went the bull. Henry guided the bull's probing organ to its goal, he gave one massive heave, then slid back down and it was all over. The animal was led back into the field and we headed down the lane for home. It was all over just as quick as that and hopefully the bull had made a meaningful deposit into my investment bank! The bull followed us wild eyed on the other side of the stone ditch. Did he have feelings for Bluebell? Do animals form that kind of attachment? I don't know, it seemed like it, but it was never going to be and we had an uneventful trip home.

'How did it go, did you have any trouble?,' my father asked anxiously.

Should I tell him? Risk his disapproval? After all the encounter wasn't my fault and I thought I handled the situation pretty well. So I told him everything that transpired with the bastard bull.

'Well, that's not good, but sure you did yer best. Did he serve her?'

'I don't think so.'

'What d'ye mean you don't think so! What were you doing? Weren't you paying attention?' he said sharply.

So I had to explain the encounter all over again in detail to his satisfaction.

'Right then. Was there anyone there with a cow before you in Kennedys?'

It was the first time I heard this question but it wouldn't be the last, and I didn't understand the significance of it.

'There was, we met Charlie Gilmartin coming down.'

This information seemed to bother him more than the encounter with the unlicensed bull. He frowned and walked away. Much later I reflected in my mind if his simple but purposeful question had something to do with the Aberdeen's slow response to Bluebell's advances.

In the succeeding months there was much to think about. I didn't believe the mongrel bull got to her but then again I couldn't be sure. There was always the possibility that she might 'miss', as cows often did, and we would have another chance to get it right. But Bluebell grazed contentedly in the weeks and months that followed her romantic interlude. We worked torturously in the meadow fields all through that wet summer: shook the hay out, made lappings when rain threatened, coaxed, teased and dried it till eventually it was saved into tall statuesque trampcocks dotted all around the meadow fields.

When the summer work was done and the hay gathered into the haggard in October, Bluebell, sleek from summer pastures, had grown fat and round. Like an expectant father almost I watched her grow big, gave her an extra armful of hay, fed her sliced turnips with a generous sprinkling of Indian meal on top, talked to her and her calf. She looked back at me and, it might be fanciful, but I think we shared a kind of empathy. She seemed to sense my anxiety and her importance to my plans. But she was always a placid animal and I suppose that is why she was loaned to me in the first place.

Summer gave way to Autumn, Autumn to Winter and the cows were once again moved to their winter quarters. Hay, so painstakingly saved during the summer months was fed to them armful by armful. The days grew short and shorter and then following the doldrum days of the winter solstice, longer again in their perpetual cycle. Bluebell continued to swell. Instead of lying down the best she could manage now was to flop ungracefully; getting up required more and more of an effort. I observed all of this sympathetically and with a stretch in the days became filled with anticipation. She was due in February and I wouldn't have long now to wait.

February 27th my mother and I had marked in the calendar last May. A few days before this and right on schedule Bluebell showed a 'springing' and drops of milk trickled from her teats. The 27th came and went and the tension increased as I impatiently awaited the birth of this my firstborn. On the morning of the 28th the calf bones were sufficiently depressed to show that the calf would arrive before nightfall. The kitchen furniture was rearranged and a fresh bed of hay laid down in anticipation of the new arrival. It would be the first calf of the year so a palpable excitement filled the air.

The day wore on, Bluebell became more and more restless and the signs of calving progressed. In the evening she lay down and began to press, then as if she changed her mind she got up again, pranced tightly as much as her tether would allow and lay down again. Thinking anxiously of something I might do that would help I left a bucket of water at her head that had been warmed by a stream of hot water from the kettle. There were several repetitions of this and as night fell the water sack became visible. For almost an hour this went on with no visible sign of progress. She pressed and moaned and bawled her distress, and then seemed to just give up the struggle. Her presses became weaker and my father who was watching very carefully made a decision:

'We better take the calf!' he said, the strain showing on his face, and then turning to me:

'What do you think, Joe, it's your calf?'

I was pleased to be asked but having very little experience could only agree.

'Alright Dad, whatever you think is best!'

He pulled a pin from the lapel of his coat, stooped and swiftly punctured the water bag. A flood of liquid spilled out.

Reaching into the opening he searched for the calf's legs and:

'I'm afraid the calf is coming wrong', he said.

I could only remember reading other people's experiences of crisis where they described time as standing still. That's how I remember it now, of time being suspended; I cannot recall if it was a minute or an hour as we groped for the calf's feet. It was a breached birth. Finding the feet we took wisps of hay in our hands the better to grip the slippery legs, and pulled. We pulled and rested, and pulled again, with all the strength we could muster — to no avail.

'Get that rope from the peg,' my father's voice was tense but calm. Tying the rope securely to the calf's feet gave us better leverage. We pulled again, the calf inched slowly out and in one final mighty effort slid on to the ground.

It was a Hereford — and it was lifeless, drowned in the womb.

On the birth of a healthy calf depended the success or failure of our family's finances. A slender thread in a delicate weave that sustained, even if only at a coping level, the welfare of the family. My first step on the road to becoming a grown-up, even a farmer, in which I had placed so much trust, was a failure: as dead as the calf itself.

Something changed forever on that day and I became more and more aware of the pitfalls, the fragilities and uncertainties, the vagaries of life lived so close to unpredictable Nature. The lifestyle of emigrants from the village who returned each year during the summer seemed infinitely more attractive, more predictable than mine ever could be.

On the threshold of a landscape and lifestyle that was rapidly and irrevocably shifting, that would see greater change than any other on the planet, I was becoming increasingly unsure of what the future might hold.

# 5

## THE HIDDEN PEOPLE

Mary Ann Donlon went to the door, looked up and down the street and seeing no sign of anyone, trimmed the wick on the lamp and put the kettle on. No light switch had ever been turned on in Inishmurray Island. There was none, nor a light bulb, or an E.S.B. pole — or for that matter running water, or a kitchen sink. These facilities wouldn't arrive in the Sligo countryside until the '60s.

Previous generations had only firelight to work by or, at best, candles. Now they had paraffin lamps. Dishes were washed in a hand basin on the kitchen table. Feet were washed in a similar vessel beside the fire. Children were bathed in a big galvanised tub when they got too big for the basin. The wastewater was thrown out on to a street that was cobblestoned and channelled to take it away. It served too as a runoff for the rainwater that came off the eaves.

A roof that was comfortably thatched, a stack of turf at the gable, a winter's supply of potatoes in clay pits in the field, a warm turf fire and a houseful of 'ramblers' to sit around it and chat on winter nights: what more could a person want out of life!

Outside in the darkness, in the deep-shaded streets of *Baile*

*Thiar* or *Baile Thoir* there existed a realm they did not fully understand — but for the most part it did not interfere with their world, nor they with it. They were at peace with this Otherworld, dimly understood. *Manntrach*, away beyond Clashmore Harbour, was a fairy place that was best left to these 'gentle people'. At *Poll a' Phíobaire* (Hole of the Piper) out to the southwest, strains of pipe music, too sweet to be played by any mortal hand, carried across the land on still frosty nights.

Distillation of the illegal whiskey known as *poitín* was an island industry. No taxes were paid to government agencies but it was a foolish man that didn't pay homage to the watchful fairy world:

'The first run that comes from the still, especially the '*dubhrach*', we take a ponger of that an' give it to the good people; that's the hidden people of Ireland.'

Dominick 'Crimley' Harte was chatting and telling stories, as he often did, to his listeners Mary Ann Donlon, her mother Catty and a few neighbours that had gathered in for a chat. It was late on a Halloween night and they were sitting around the fire anxiously awaiting the return of the rest of the family that had gone out earlier that day to the mainland for supplies.

While Crimley talked he sliced thin shavings off a bar of plug tobacco with his penknife. Having peeled off enough to fill his pipe he held the flakes in the palm of his left hand and steadily ground them into a finer mix with the heel of his right. Peel and grind. Peel and grind steadily while little by little his stories unfolded. Occasionally at a turning point in the narrative he would pause, cock his head to one side, close one eye and fix the listeners with a steady, good-humoured gaze. The preparation, the pauses, the story: they were an unaffected kitchen theatre. It was all part of the performance, an inherent gift, and his spell was such that no one interrupted, even during the pauses; they were themselves filled with import and meaning. There was all the time in the world and the listeners hung on his every word.

Now he paused and pulling an old stump of a blackened clay pipe out of his dungarees, filled the bowl. Worming the tobacco down with his thumb he packed it methodically. Taking a live coal from the fire he held it to the mix and drew until the tobacco took light and little clouds of smoke puffed from the corner of his mouth, lingered, and drifted away up the chimney. The glow from the coal highlighted a deeply lined and rugged countenance that sparkled with good humour. Decorated with an imposing moustache it was topped by the grease-stained peak of a countryman's cap pulled low over intense blue eyes. Age and hard living had served only to give character to his face — a face that must have had film star good looks in his youth.

'We'd fill the ponger an' we'd go out an we'd lave it on a big rock called *Clocha Breacha*. We'd bring the ponger with us, the first run, an' we'd say: *"Seogin, seogin, seogin sidhe; seogin, seogin sidhe, Cead mile failte rud air a bi seachain seo"*[6].

If we didn't give the first drop away to the fairies something was sure to happen to the run. Anyone that didn't give it

---

[6] First part is calling the fairies, then: 'hundred thousand welcomes to anything that is in this house.'

away, the first drop, they were either caught with the police on the mainland or it was stole on them. But the party that always kept up the oul' custom, nothing happened them, an' they got treble the value of the *poitín* they had in their barrels. Whatever was the cause of it — . '

The clock chiming the dead hour of midnight interrupted Crimley's conversation. On the last stroke they were startled by a loud knocking on the door. In those times that was a very strange thing, because doors were always on the latch. People didn't knock. Neighbour as well as family just lifted the latch and walked in.

Mary Ann went to the door half afraid on account of the strangeness of the knock.

'*Ce'n tart amach?*' says she, 'Who's out there?'

Irish was the only language that was spoken on the island. There was a barely audible reply. She couldn't quite make it out but thought it sounded like it was one of the neighbours. Turning around to the gathering in the corner she said:

'Oh, I think it's one of the neighbours outside. What'll I do?'

'Well what are ye waiting for,' says Crimley. 'Open the door why don't ye!'

Mary Ann opened the door and a faint light from the oil lamp dimly lit three indistinct figures standing on the threshold. She was a bit taken aback that there was three people there but nevertheless not wanting to show her concern she invited them in.

'Come in out of the cold,' she said, '*Tá failte romhaibh*, you're welcome.'

At that the three women stepped into the light. They were in bare feet and dressed in the island fashion of the time with red skirts and red petticoats. Two of them had plaid shawls around their shoulders. The other woman wore a knitted cap called a *bairéad*. It had a distinctive crocheted linen border and a ribbon for tying under the chin. It was in the old style that Crimley recognised from seeing it in pictures. Around this woman's shoulders was draped a black knitted shawl.

There was bewilderment on the faces of those gathered around the fireside when they saw the three women come in the door. They knew everyone on the island but they hadn't a notion who any one of these women were. There were no boats out but the one island boat that had gone to the mainland, so they couldn't have come in from there. Although watchful of what the visitor's intention might be the strangers were made welcome anyway and given a seat by the fire. 'Better to keep the bad dog with you,' was an old country saying.

'Wait now till I get you something to eat,' offered Mary Ann, in case they had come a long way and maybe were hungry. Country people were very hospitable then and even though having little themselves on account of being often marooned from the mainland, they would share whatever they had.

'No,' said the oldest of the three right away. That was the woman with the *bairéad*. 'We only came here because we want to warn you about what you do at night here.'

Crimley had been staring hard at the women and still couldn't figure them out, who they were or where they came from. Were they from Killawaddy on the mainland? He had heard they were a queer lot in that place. He didn't see why strangers, no matter where they were from, should come barging in an island door and give ultimatums:

'Where are ye from?' he bristled.

'Not far from yerself,' says the elderly woman right back to him.

They weren't expecting that kind of cheek from the women. The least they would look for was a civil answer. After all they were intruders in the house and better manners might be expected of them. Increasingly anxious of what was to come, they were yet at the same time curious to know more about the strange visitors and what in God's name had brought them there. Their faces in deep shade because of the hoods and shawls, there was something dangerously unsettling about the three women. One of the children in the group began to sob quietly.

The situation didn't take a feather out of Crimley. He feared nothing from human, fairy or ghost, natural or supernatural.

'Arrah, musha,' he says, calm as ye like, 'not far from us? That'd be the country outside a few miles away on the mainland.'

'No," says the old one, 'nearer than that to ye. We see you every day in the week but you don't see us. So we're near enough to ye. I can't say any more. Ye'll have to figure it out for yourselves now what I mean.'

Crimley began to ponder:

'I'm thinking I do,' he says, 'ye belong to the good people.'

'No matter who we belong to,' was the answer, 'it's neither

here nor there; we didn't come to do you any harm. You do leave things out for us on a set night. Ye lave the water for us, ye lave the drop of whiskey for us on the doorstep at Christmas, ye lave the cake on the table at Halloween, an' we appreciate that, but you have one bad habit," she says.'

'After the night falls,' says the woman, 'you have a habit of going to the door an' ye take a basin of oul' slop wash ye might have in the house, an ye open the door an ye slosh it right out. That's alright, we don't mind that, but ye never say:

*'Chugaibh, chugaibh, chugaibh an t-uisge salach'.*[7]

Her words immediately put everyone on the defensive. How could these strange women have known that? They looked at one another in astonishment; yes, they were indeed guilty as charged and knew the woman was right. How many times had Crimley told them to say these few words as a warning to avoid drenching or giving offence to ghosts or fairies that might be passing in the pitch black of the island night? And particularly on Halloween when everyone knew the graveyards were open and spirits wandering at will.

'Now I want to ask you a request," the stranger continued, 'never do that again. Many a night ye threw your dirty water on some of your own people, after dark. We know ye didn't do it intentionally but you often done it. I'm warning you now, don't ever do it again.

So now, our work here is done, we thank ye for the heat of the fire and for your hospitality but we can't take anything. We have to go, and now, remember, won't you take that advice

---

7 Here's to you, here's to you, here's to you the dirty water.

from me,' she said looking around sharply at the anxious faces before her.

Bidding her companions to follow she turned on her heel, lifted the latch, and the little group went out of the door as swiftly and silently as they had come.

Crimley and the women in the house immediately rushed to the door to see if they could find out which direction the visitors had gone. Quick as they were the women had vanished. Vanished as if they had melted into the ground or disappeared into thin air — and as far as anyone knows neither health nor hair of them ever was seen again!

# 6

## THE MATCHMAKER AND THE PILL

Lunch boxes by their side, each man wrapped in his own thoughts, Danny and his workmates were on their sullen Monday morning way to work. It was a familiar daily journey from University Ave. in the Bronx to a construction site on West 4<sup>th</sup> St. in lower Manhattan

'This is no life for any man!' Danny O'Malley declared suddenly right out of the blue!

His voice was barely audible above the subway's rattle as it swayed and screeched, hurtling frantically through the dark and winding labyrinths beneath Manhattan Island. Everyone jammed together, standing room only, swaying in unison with the other straphanging rush hour commuters: butchers, bakers, candlestick makers.

'What's up with ye now?' Seamus Muldoon responded nudging his neighbour with a big smirk on his face. Danny's longing for home was well known to them and they could see by his countenance he was in a particularly sour mood this morning.

'Haven't ye a great time of it, making money hand over fist and out every night on the town. Sure home was never like this!' Seamus continued with a secretive wink.

'Maybe it's as well it wasn't,' Danny snapped irritably. 'What's it all about? That's all anyone ever thinks about in this country is work, work, work and money, money, money, from morning till night. There has to be more to life than this. The worth of a man's life is not measured in money!'

It was true indeed. Danny had worked hard, very hard, and done extremely well for himself. Finally he had come to the realisation that it is the nature of man, having conquered the summit he is on, to strive for the other peaks stretching out and beyond the horizon.

'Oh my! Aren't we touchy this morning! What you need to do is stop carousing and find a good woman to settle down with that'll raise a houseful of childer for ye,' Muldoon the perennial bachelor offered.

This suggestion was like a red rag to a bull to Danny who had a jaundiced view of American woman.

'An' what would you know no more than the priest?' he responded indignantly. And where, might I ask, would you get a good woman over here? You wouldn't know what to do to please American women, most of them have been around the block more than once, they're painted from head to toe and quick as a flash you'd be divorced and out on the side of the road if you said one word out of place.'

'Well, if that's the way you feel about it why don't you go back to Killawaddy and find one of these wholesome Irish girls that you're always talking about! Sure with the bags of money you have you'd be a great catch.'

'Why don't you go back to Killawaddy? Oh, why don't you go back to Killawaddy.' Danny parroted. 'Wasn't I there long enough working poor land on a small farm for all I made out of it! You could lift a scraw at Killawaddy and it'd come with you the entire way to Tubbercurry. Try and grow crops on that!'

'Well, sure you don't have to stay there. Once you tie the knot you can bring her back here and have the best of both worlds! And when you're at it you could bring a few more of them back with you! It's something that's badly needed around here,' Muldoon laughed.

That gave Danny food for thought. Indeed and the notion to venture home had crossed his mind many a time without any prompting. It was just about fifteen years since he had first set foot in New York and there wasn't a day since he left Ireland that he didn't pine for the friends and the family he left behind. The perception that people who never leave home love it better than those who go is mistaken. Often it is chance or inertia that keeps the homebodies there. The people who live the farthest away, those that circumstances and the necessity of earning a living have displaced, it is they that cherish and appreciate home the most. To them it is a special place that, when they lay their head to rest at night, inspires their dreams; thoughts of it is the harbour to where their heart flies, the sanctuary where their soul finds rest.

And so it was with Danny. When he talked about 'home' — which was often — it was Killawaddy was on his mind not his apartment in the Bronx. Although doing well for himself in his adopted land he still missed the good neighbours, fresh air, open fields, and rugged mountains of memory. The longer he was away the greener they became.

Prior to emigrating he had worked diligently on his father's farm from dawn to close of day. Sometime in the future, when his father passed on, he knew it would all be his. The seasons came and went, year followed dutiful year, and at the end of each year he was no better off than he was at the beginning. Gradually it dawned on him that that's the way it was and the way it was always going to be. There was no future in it for him. Most of his friends had already come to the same conclusion and, one by one, had taken the boat or plane for greener pastures. Growing daily more restless Danny, despite his father's pleadings, left his home in Killawaddy, Co. Sligo in the late '50s in search of a better life.

When Danny got to New York he heard there was big money to be made on the construction sites. Fresh off the farm he had absolutely no trade or training but that was a small detail that had a ready solution. This business of starting at the bottom was a cod; he was long enough at the bottom; this time he was going to start at the top. That's how things were done in the 'Big Apple'.

The construction industry in New York was run by Italians and controlled by an unseen Mafia. Unseen that is if you minded your own business. One shop steward, who should have known better, didn't and got shot in the buttocks in an elevator on his way to work. His rear end, the rumour went, was not the intended target but he had spun around quickly when the gun was fired. There were lines in the Big Apple that you didn't cross. The Italians might have the whip hand on contracts and jobs but the Irish had a trump card: they controlled the unions — and they looked after their own!

Both nationalities, being first or second generation immigrants, understood each other very well, enough to share a common dislike. If there was no mutual admiration between them then there was at least a marriage of convenience. The 'Guineas', as they were mockingly nicknamed, needed workers and the 'Micks' needed jobs.

Carpenters Local Union 608 controlled the Manhattan district. That's where the big money was. Gabriel Cassidy was the business rep that looked after the Sligo men. He could always shoehorn a few lads fresh off the boat onto a construction site as journeymen carpenters. The work there was rough and if they were good workers and quick to learn they could do well enough for themselves. Of course there was a fistful of money to be paid over for the union card but once that little matter was taken care of and you asked no questions and kept your nose clean, it was plain sailing.

In the early years of his arrival Danny had come to love New York, loved the hustle and bustle as he and his workmates scrambled and built from first light; sawed and hammered in a frenzy of creation creating floor by floor an emerging skyscraper, shaping a city. Uptown the Empire State and Chrysler buildings, tallest structures in the world, magnificently reflected the morning sun as it climbed out of the East River; painting equally with gold the windows of the rich man and the poor; startling awake the homeless tramps in that nether world of shivering cardboard mattresses. Southwards there was the mighty arm of the Statue of Liberty holding her lamp to the clouds. Sirens wailed in the canyons of the city that never sleeps, tugboats rushed upriver and down emitting excited blares and whistles. The sights and sounds touched the heart's core of him. 'Yes,' he exulted, 'yes, this is the heart of creation.' New York, particularly as it revealed itself to him in the breaking day, was overwhelming: the hub and epicentre of the Western world!

※

The train stopped at Washington Square. One flock of faceless, hurrying butchers, bakers and candlestick makers exited; another got on; the train, screeching and clackedy-clacking on its iron rails sped off and disappeared dragon-like through a dark tunnel with its human cargo. Danny's step was slow and thoughtful. He fell behind his friends as they walked the five blocks to a maze of concrete and excavated earth that was their place of work. As he walked he contemplated with gloomy cynicism the foregone conclusions of the monotonous day that lay ahead The shop stewards whistle blew and like workers in an ant colony, or robots activated by the shrill sound, men swarmed to their appointed places. Danny coupled the timbers and tightened the iron clamps on the wooden shuttering for a series of columns that, when the concrete was poured and set, would support the massive weight of the concrete slab that would form the next floor above. On top of that would go another set of columns and then another floor above that again and so on for twenty, thirty, forty floors, maybe sixty or more, one floor every two days. There was nothing small in this town, or slow. If you had a strong back, a head for heights and the heart of a lion this ant colony would always need ants.

His heart wasn't in his work this morning though, and his mind a tumble of thoughts. Just as the urge to leave Ireland grew day by day in the heart of him fifteen years ago, now it had him in its grip again — but this time the desire was to return to Killawaddy. New York for him had lost its appeal. The freedom and excitement he felt when he first arrived was long gone. And truth to tell there was another less attractive side to this city that became increasingly apparent as the years went by. He recalled the first time his cousins brought him down the West Side Highway to admire the sights and lights of the 'Great White Way'. To their great surprise he saw only the anonymity and, yes, even loneliness in the tens of thousands of souls behind the bright lights in huge monolithic blocks of concrete and steel — but did anyone matter to anyone else? What of this one lighted window, this pinpoint of light among the multitudes? What heartbreak or joy or misery was concealed within? What were they different than rats in a labyrinth scurrying to and fro?

His uncle had bought him coffee and a jelly doughnut at a diner on 44th and Broadway. His wondering eyes beheld a frayed formica counter and cockroaches behind the coffeemaker at the back of a cramped and shabby space.

It was a city of fierce contrasts that he had come to love and hate in equal measure. The longer he lived here the more he realised that the umbilical cord that connected him to home still held him fast. Certain sights and smells could still trigger off homesickness — like the day he smelled the new mown hay in Central Park. At home it was a good and easy-going life with the friends and neighbours he knew well and had grown up with. Trouble was that of work there was plenty, of reward very little.

Over here there was work aplenty and opportunities galore. Nowhere on this earth however is there a perfect peace, a place where all the things we want and desire come together in perfect harmony. His pockets were full now but his heart: empty. Increasingly he felt that the 'melting pot' of ethnic groups that was New York just wasn't for him. It was fine, but it wasn't home. There was no sense of belonging. And it was no melting pot either. There was Guineas and Wops, Spicks and Micks, Kikes and Polacks, Niggers and Squareheads.

'Did you hear the one about the tanks the Guineas invented during the war?'

'No.'

'It had one forward speed and four in reverse!'

'Oh very good! Do you know what a Kike picnic is?

'No, go on, tell me!'

'It's ten Kikes sitting around a septic tank with long straws!'

'What are you doing for Paddy's Day, Mick?'

'Ah, I suppose I'll go to the parade on Fifth Ave.'

'Did you go downtown to City Hall?'

'No. What for?'

'Oh, to get your ass painted green! Ha ha ha...'

Every nationality had their own turf and felt *they* were superior to everyone else. There was Germantown and Chinatown and Little Italy and God knows what Othertown, and there was no love lost between the communities! There was no Irishtown, but outside of the Irish sections of Bainbridge and the Bronx Danny felt like a fish out of water. For him New York had become an endless routine of drudgery and the banality of work. The roar of the city and the conceits of the Great White Way were nothing more than a confusion of babbling tongues. Like lemmings in their rush to the sea the tramping feet and blank expressionless faces rushed past him. Never an eye or lip returned his smile; a friendly greeting drew only a curious stare. Nowhere could loneliness be more painful than in the crowded hubbub of a city street. The hurrying, rushing feet, the anxious faces. Anonymous, heartless, bereft of humanity. Each one cocooned in his or her own anxiety. Like statues by some miracle brought to life, soulless and lifeless as the unyielding marble.

The roar of the city was a roar of greed; bleak and soulless, its inhabitants were androids controlled from space by alien beings, scurrying to and fro; it was the fumbling in the greasy till, the cry and scramble of a million hopes that to him had become increasingly irrelevant There was a growing emptiness within him. He was comfortably well off, but man needs a mate, the years were moving on and he wasn't going to find that here...

'Nail the fuckin' thing! Nail it before it rots!'

Muldoon's indignant bellow broke into Danny's reverie.

'What the fuck is wrong with you today? What do ye think yer getting' paid for?'

'Ah, fuck you too, take it easy; you're as bad as the rest of them, nothing bothering you but work and money. Bucks like you think ye own the company.'

'Yer getting paid, and well paid, to do a day's work so me boy ye'd better knuckle down and get on with it. You're not indispensable. There's plenty more where you came from!'

'Ye can't take it with ye, and ye know what! You can stick yer job where the monkey stuck the nuts. I'm goin' home.'

'You're what?' Muldoon was incredulous!

'You heard it, I'm for home!'

'Well, you're a bigger bollocks than I thought. That'll be the day you'll regret, pal! Distance is giving you rose tinted glasses. I seen the likes of you before and they were back here with their tail between their legs within a year. Tell you what, before you make up your mind I'll do you a favour, I'll put you in touch with some other heroes that went home and had to come back here again. That'll sober ye up!'

Realising his workmate's concern for him was genuine, that night he rang the numbers Muldoon gave him and listened carefully to what they had to say.

'Well, it's grand when you go home for a holiday, everyone loves you, but when you go for good and start lookin' for a job or they think you have a bit of money the tune changes awful quick!' one said.

'When you reach a certain plateau in life,' another explained, 'one is not going to settle for less in Ireland.'

Plateaus! Danny thought shaking his head when he got off the phone. Plateaus! Isn't it high notions some get! What in the name of God were they expecting! Plateaus in Ireland? If it was 'plateaus' they were after then Ireland wasn't the place to look! Less would do him! Danny's father had died a few years ago and left him the place. His brother Malachy, having no taste for farming had got himself a job with the County Council. The money was small but enough to build a modest house on the outskirts of the town and he was now a happily married man. The home they had grown up in however was going to rack and ruin and Danny felt responsible for that. It seemed that no matter where you went in this world things weren't going to be perfect. He had a bit of money saved, enough to build up the farm again when he got back, with a bit to spare, and sure you never know, the woman he'd marry might even come with a bit of a dowry as well. He had finally made up his mind. All kinds of possibilities beckoned. He was going home. Happy now and light-headed with joy, he headed off to the travel agent in the morning where he bought a one-way ticket to Shannon.

Winging his way homeward he leaned back in his seat, closed his eyes and allowed his thoughts to turn to the home and village he would soon set eyes on again. Could it be that Killawaddy would be nothing more now than a lost village in the mists and clouds of an American induced green-tinted imagination? Someone once said 'you can never go home again'. He was going home but had he changed? Had home changed? Would the conversations with which he was once so familiar have any relevance for him anymore? Were there two Danny O'Malleys totally unrelated: one, the eager, impulsive youth that left Ireland all those years ago; and now the older, more experienced man. Did they have anything in common? More importantly would his old flame Peggy be glad to see him.

Except for a letter and card at Christmas he wasn't much at the writing and had gradually lost touch with her and with the affairs of the village.

Arriving in Shannon he looked around for his brother who promised to meet him. Immediately he noticed a suspicious looking character with a grey beard following him and was wary. There were lots of shady types like that around the airport in New York; he wasn't expecting it in Shannon.

'Hello Danny.'

He was on his guard immediately. 'Streetwise' they called it in the Bronx and he ventured a cautious 'Hello?' in reply.

'I'll throw your case in the car.'

Now he peered more intently at the strange figure and, Christ, he thought incredulously could this be my own brother Malachy! The figure in front of him was an oldster: fat, paunchy and bald as an egg, but a with a pleasant enough face and two twinkly eyes peering from the depths of a great beard. This was not the young athletic brother he had left behind.

'Did ye not know me?'

He didn't, and years later when the beard was shaved he swore it wasn't his brother that came out from behind it. It was not the brother he knew, and he never again saw the childhood face he remembered so well.

Home to Sligo they travelled, through Galway and Clare, past fieldstone walls, grassy acres and heather bogs. Ireland had become mechanised in his absence and where previously men and women had worked the hayfields with scythe, rake and fork now he saw tractors, shakers and New Holland balers.

The impersonal roar of Massey Ferguson's diesel monsters had replaced the clip clop of Clydesdale and Irish draught. Reaching Killawaddy he looked around for more changes. There were many, but some clung to the old ways. There was 'Wee' Brian Mc Gloin coming up the road with his spade worn away at the tip and polished silver from constant use. His leathery face, deeply lined, wizened and elf-like from constant exposure to sun, wind and rain, cackled into a broad grin.

'Ah, Christ is it yerself is in it? Well I'd know yer oul' skin on a bush,' he greeted cheerily, extending a calloused, earth-stained hand. 'Well yer a thousand times welcome! Ye haven't changed a bit. Where do the years go?'

'Thanks Brian! You haven't changed a bit yourself.'

He had — both of them had — but it wouldn't be just the thing to say right now. Now it was time for the niceties; assessment, analysis and speculation would come later, out of earshot of the analysed party.

'Are you on holiday, or are ye going to stay a while?'

'Home for good, Brian. I'm sick of America, time to come back where I belong. Tired of the bright lights.'

'Well, I'll tell you the truth, you're a foolish man. There's nothing here for anyone only hard work. I love the bright lights meself.'

This last comment greatly amused Danny as Brian had never left home. What he knew of bright lights would have come from stories told to him by emigrants home on holidays exaggerating to impress. Like many a man before him who had never left home Brian often regretted he had not done so while the fire of youth was in full flood.

'How's the farming going?'

'Ahhh, same as ever Danny, it never changed. Killin' time and bafflin' hunger as usual. Did ye ever see a rich wormcutter yet!'

'Well, it's good to see you anyway Brian. Why don't ye come over for a ramble soon as I get settled in.'

'Well I'll do that surely, no lie nor doubt, and I couldn't be more pleased to see you than if I won the sweepstakes!'

Yes indeed it was good to be home.

Walking down the little lane to the home he left all those years ago, tears of joy and sadness stung Danny's eyes: joy to be back again, sadness at the silence, the overgrown garden, the profusion of weeds in the cobblestones. Gazing intently at the once familiar scene he could hear again, faintly in the summer breeze, the sound of laughing children, the lowing of cows, his mother calling him to dinner. And, yes, there it was, beyond the ragged fields, the restless ocean waves still tumbling tirelessly on the cliffs at *Ros na Rí* in great eruptions of foam and spray. A savage splendour. He thought of his father and all the generations gone before who had looked out on this same unchanging scene, observed the same sights that filled his senses now. Or had they? Had separation brought to Danny a different perception, a keener awareness, perhaps a greater appreciation of this wild beauty undimmed now by the endless, unprofitable toil and care of former times? Surrounded every day by such exotic beauty perhaps they never saw it.

'Ye can't ate a view y'know!' locals would wryly respond to compliments on the scenery.

There was nothing to show that these men and women had ever existed — except perhaps for the silent stone ditches that squared the fields. Each stone carefully picked, placed and fitted to its neighbour with infinite skill. Apart from that each year's work was ploughed under by the next. These walls were the only nameless, wordless monuments to a 'bold peasantry' that had passed that way.

Standing motionless, Danny felt drawn into a spiritual connection with these ghosts and their way of life. In a confusion of emotions he wept; wept for them, for the hardships they suffered, for their puny existence — and yet they possessed something that he had lost: a connection to and an affection for the soil. They knew its strengths and failures, how to tease and coax the most out of it as if it were a living person. Holding his head in his hands, his shoulders shook, tears flooded his eyes. He wept shamelessly for himself, for the stolen years he had spent away from this land he loved, where his roots ran so deep. At thirty-seven years of age, having spent his formative years in search of wealth, had he missed something much more important?

He stepped cautiously into the kitchen, a kitchen that seemed so much smaller than he had remembered it. A dull light struggled through the cracked and cobwebbed windows lighting a filthy, stone-flagged floor. There in the chimney corner was the armchair where his father had spent his declining years, where he had watched, vulnerable and hopeless, as Danny walked out the door into a new life. There on the other gable, little changed except for a covering of dust, was the open dresser with its array of plates, cups and bowls.

Enough then! He was home. Life is built not on regrets but new beginnings. There was work to be done. This place had to be whipped into shape. For weeks he cleaned, weeded and scrubbed. By force of will and energy he breathed life back into the heart of the four walls and everything within: a fire burned brightly on the hearthstone; a plume of turf smoke rose triumphantly from the chimney; the front door stood once more welcomingly ajar. Transformed, the house and outbuildings looked again like a place where a man might want to live.

Now he turned his attention to the fields, fallen like the house and sheds into ruin. The country was on the mend everyone said and if a man bought right he could do well. What was lacking before he left home was money. 'It takes money to make money' he often heard his father, who had little enough of it, say. Now he had a nice nest egg. If he spent it wisely he could have a good life.

His neighbour on the other side of the hill, Cathail Canavan, took 'The Yank' under his wing. He loaned him the tractor when he needed it, gave him advice on liming and manuring. Taking him to the cattle marts he showed him the ropes of buying and selling. Street fairs had gone out of fashion while Danny was away and a different kind of craft was now required. On Cathail's advice he bought eight in-calf heifers at Ballinagaddy mart, renovated the byres and barns and put up a new hayshed. Within a few short months cattle grazed the fields; a flock of hens pecked around the yard; a drove of fine sheep dotted the hillside. His newly acquired border collie loped and panted alongside him darting here and there keeping the sheep in check.

Danny's return was akin to the limpet that lives on the seashore. On the flood tide it releases its grip on the rock to forage. On the ebb it must return to the exact spot, the only tiny place on all the seashore to where its shell is moulded, the only place where it fits. Truly Danny was back among his own people, he had rediscovered the niche where he justly belonged and life was good!

Yet there was one thing missing: a woman with which to share his life, bed and fortune! Thinking to himself that '*A burnt coal is easy kindled*' and having fond memories of Peggy, his flame of former days, he sought news of her. This too had changed and he quickly discovered she now had a husband and a houseful of children. Reflecting only briefly on this setback he turned his attentions elsewhere: 'no use crying over spilt milk' and he let it be quietly known that he was on the lookout for a woman. This could be the most difficult hurdle of all as no price or plan could be put on affairs of the heart.

He was a good-looking fellow with strong square jaws and bright piercing blue eyes set in a ruddy face as honest as it was handsome. With his build he could have been a boxer and neighbours often remarked on his stature and the grand garda he would have made. His height was crowned by a great shock of black hair; the few grey hairs emerging at the temples just enough to impart an air of distinction, and indeed heads turned when he went to a fair or a dance.

'A fine cut of a man,' the neighbours agreed, 'but innocent in the ways of the world. A bit soft where women are concerned.'

Although never having mastered the foxtrots, slow waltzes and quicksteps that cut a dash at the local dancehall he decided to give it a go anyway. Once he got past the introductory, 'Where are ye from?' and 'D'ye come here often,' he floundered. Danny was too unskilled in the art of seduction, the glib chat that turned the ladies' heads, to be entirely happy in that environment. What he wanted to talk about were the things that interested him, the solid things in life: his cattle, his home, his delight in the ordinary pleasures of the countryside, which they, never having left, took for granted. What use was a foxtrot when a cow was calving? Or a quickstep at making a bargain on a fair day! Many's the good woman lived to rue the day her head was turned by smart talk and nimble feet.

Some of the candidates were past their prime, some too young, and the most desirable already off the market, married and beyond reach. Had Danny come to pluck his apples too late?

'Ah, sure you have no sense at all, aren't you well enough off as you are,' Malachy advised him one evening as the two of them sat around the fire in the kitchen where they had both grown up. Danny was a sentimentalist and although having fitted out the house with modern appliances had kept the flagstones, open hearth and crane crook. The chat had got around to Danny's marital ambitions

'Well, if ye don't marry when you have no sense sure I suppose ye'd never marry at all,' Danny offered. 'The thing about it is that I have the cage now, but I still don't have the bird,' he laughed.

'That's true enough' Malachy agreed, 'but sure if you're that determined then what you need to do is go and get yourself a matchmaker. What about "Cork the Bottle"? Why don't you have a word with him? He's a champion of hard cases like yourself — and he knows everyone in the countryside!'

'Cork the Bottle'? Who's he? And anyway, aren't matchmakers a thing of the past?'

'Ahh, who's Cork the Bottle! You've been away too long. Don't you remember Willie McElduff! Mind you, you could do worse than have a chat with him,' Malachy said thoughtfully spitting a stream of yellow tobacco juice into the ashes piled up at the side of the fire: 'Most men choose women for all the wrong reasons. Most women know exactly what they want. Men rarely do. If they get their hands on a pair of knickers they're only thinking of one thing. That's the bait. The matchmaker stands aside from all that emotional stuff, the fire and the passion, and makes a decision based on what matters: reason and commonsense. He'll take a bottle of whiskey with him, that's traditional, go to the house and have a sensible chat with the girl's father. They'll look at your land and discuss what you're worth and then agree on how much of a dowry the girl should bring in to match that. There's a couple of fine women down there in Lenehans of Tournawalla. You could start there'

Christ! Malachy, his own brother: what an unlikely philosopher.

'Well, you have a low opinion of human nature,' Danny responded with a laugh.

'High or low it's an opinion anyway, and maybe you might come round to it yourself yet.'

'Ah, yer talking rubbish man! A matchmaker is a last resort, it's for losers, I'll take my chances the old fashioned way.'

Still, the thought had taken root and gave Danny much to think about. His brother always had a steady head on him as could be seen from his own choices in life: modest, but comfortable enough in a middle class kind of way. Danny had achieved success in a different manner, if success it was. As far as material things were concerned he had more money than Malachy would ever have. But Malachy was settled and fat and contented.

Contented!

And what was wrong with that? What did it take to make a man happy, to bring fulfilment? It was the riddle of the ages. For every man there was a different answer. For some it was the conquering of Everest or to be first at the North Pole or to cross the ocean single-handed. For men of modest ambitions like Malachy it was the simple home life. Now that he had travelled and seen a bit of the world, for Danny it was a woman to share what he had — for rich or for poorer. If he had that he would be contented and never ask for more.

Pondering Malachy's advice he decided to take it and, plucking up his courage, went next day to see Willie McElduff or 'Cork' as he was known — but not to his face of course:

'I'm told there's a couple of single women down there in Lenehans in Tournawalla. Do ye know them Willie? I might throw me hat in the ring there. Would ye help me?'

'Oh I heard of them alright. I'm afraid ye'd be takin' your pigs to a bad market there, Danny. Sure them is two small wee women. Why don't you go up to Knockbeg, there's a family of Murtaghs there with three fine women in the house, they're bigger, you'll do better. They'll be glad to see you coming. Look out for the father though, Big Mick, he's a rare one, the kind of bucko'd take the eye out of yer head and try to convince ye you were better off without it.'

'Sure don't I know them! Isn't one of them Anastasia? I had a wee chat with her at the last fair in Kinlough and ye know, I think she liked me. Will ye come over with me?'

'Ah, sure I will, you get the bottle and let me know when you're ready.'

Willie made it his business to run into Anastasia, accidentally of course, a few days later and after exchanging a few pleasantries mentioned Danny:

'Ye know he has no one in the house but himself,' he says to her. 'It can be lonely and a bit o' company would be nice at times.'

'That's the Yank isn't it? I don't mind,' says she noncommittally, 'Sure we could see about it.'

'Will ye ate sweets?'

'I will.'

That was a good sign, so Cork went off and bought biscuits and sweets for her.

They sat down to eat and after a while:

'Do you know what we'll do,' he says, 'I'll bring Danny over to the house one of these days and we'll fix it up!'

'I'm willing,' she says, 'there's enough in our house, three brothers and three sisters. I think I'd be satisfied.' she says.

Cork the Bottle could hardly contain his excitement when he brought the news to Danny. Danny was ecstatic, Cork sent word ahead to Murtagh's and on the following Sunday evening the two men took their bicycles and headed off down the road for Knockbeg.

When they got to Murtaghs there was a great welcome for the two men. Introducing himself to the father, 'Big' Mick, Cork introduced Danny. Danny was impressed as Mick was even more remarkable in person than any account of him had described: an imposing big hulk with mad eyes, square jaws and hair growing wild out of every orifice. The women, Priscilla, Anastasia and Kate, threw shy glances at the visitors. They had heard about the Yank from Killawaddy and here he was now in the flesh!

It was the custom then when you went matchmaking to a place to take the girl on your knees that you intended to marry. The light in the house was poor, being a paraffin lamp, and Danny a bit shortsighted. He peered into the gloom and couldn't make out which one it was he had come for.

'Which one of them is it?' he nudged Cork with his elbow.

There were three of them in the lower room and with the poor light and having only met her once he didn't know which one to go for. The women, Priscilla, Anastasia and Kate peeked shyly around the door at the visitors.

'Arrah, God blasht it,' says Cork, 'how could ye not know which of them it is? Didn't you see her at the fair?'

Someone started up an accordeon, and with the noise and confusion and the poor light Danny still couldn't figure out which of the girls to go for. Cork's reputation as a matchmaker was not for nothing; he wasn't going to be bested and soon hit on a plan.

'The best thing we can do is I'll announce: "Danny has a notion of Anastasia, come down Anastasia and sit on Danny's knees".

All heads turned expectantly to the room. There was silence for a moment, then down she came to a patter of applause. Cork left the two of them to chat and engaged 'Big' Mick in conversation. Cork soon deduced that Mick liked what he saw in Danny and would be eager to make a match. He didn't say that of course and tried not to show it but Cork the Bottle was a shrewd man that could size a situation up very quickly. There would be business done here. Things were going well. Very well indeed.

'Would ye put the kettle on there girls, these men came a long way to see us and we can't send them home the way they came!'

To Cork he said: 'We'll have the cup of tea first and then yourself, meself and Danny can have a chat. I suppose ye have the bottle with ye, ye sly hoor!'

'Of course I do, sure where would ye be going without it!'

Danny felt at ease in the house. Chatting with the women while they were fussing with the tea, he couldn't take his eyes off the fair-haired Anastasia. Her face and complexion had an openness and a transparency through which shone a soul without blemish. A man could lose himself in such a face and flirty smiling eyes. Her shy glance hinted that she maybe liked him too. The tea was served with thick cuts of soda bread, the three men and the few neighbours lashed into it. The ladies, as was customary on such occasions, retired to the parlour, or would have if Big Mick had one, but they made do with the upper bedroom as a refuge instead.

After the meal Cork with a flourish produced a bottle of *poitín*, Big Mick got three glasses and filled them up. Drinking to each other's health the ice was soon broken, the men pulled their chairs closer to the table and soon fell into reasonably comfortable conversation. Cork and Big Mick were like two fighting cocks, circling, weighing each other up, fencing with banalities about the weather and the price of cattle; the first of which was never good enough and the second of which was never high enough. The opening round over Cork got right into it:

'Well Mick,' he started, 'I'm a man of few words and it doesn't take me long to make up me mind. If it's alright with you and if she's willing Danny here would be very happy to have Anastasia. He's a good man, none better, he has a few pound saved and a nice place over in Killawaddy and I think she'd be happy there.'

'By God yer quick off the mark alright,' Mick replied, 'but some things are better taken slowly and maybe this is one of them. Didn't ye often hear it said, "Marry in haste, repent at your leisure?"'

In the short space of time since they had met, Mick figured he had the measure of Danny and, regardless of Cork the Bottles negotiating powers, felt he could strike a good bargain here. No doubt about it, it was past time the women were married off. He often complained to the neighbours that 'a byreful of old cows or a houseful of daughters would keep any man poor.' He had heard the Yank was a soft touch and now having met him was convinced of it. There was no end to the foolishness of men where women were concerned.

'Well ye know Willie,' Big Mick Murtagh continued, 'it's always the oldest girl that gets married off out of a house first. You're long enough in the game to know that. It stands to reason. That'd be Priscilla. And fair play to her ye wouldn't get a better woman anywhere in Sligo, or Ireland for that matter.'

'Well I'm not faulting her in any way at all,' Cork soothed, 'but how am I going to tell Danny that. He has his heart set on Anastasia and he's mooning away about "the minute meself and Anastasia set eyes on each other I could see it was meant to be." And maybe it was. On top of that you know right well he's a good catch! C'mon we'll have another pull outa the bottle here and settle the details'

Danny was quiet, he didn't like Cork baring his soul to this wily old gorilla of a man but there was a lot at stake here. This was no small matter. What he was doing was choosing a partner for the rest of his life. He felt he hadn't many chances left and only one chance to get it right.

'Oh! Meant to be, was it? My but you're the quare one,' Big Mick guffawed. 'Trouble with this fella is he was too long away in Yankeeland, there's nothing meant to be around these parts!'

Big Mick explained the great girl Anastasia was, how lonely

the house would be without her, all the extra work there would be when she left, how much the other girls would miss her and a whole host of other misfortunes that would befall the house when his darling left. As well as that it wouldn't be fair to make her feel she was being passed over — no it wouldn't do at all. And so on it went.

In his scheming heart he knew Lady Luck had come in the door to him today, he had a fish on the hook and he was determined to land him.

Cork the Bottle stuck to his guns. Giving the liquor a while to settle he waxed eloquent about Danny's virtues, the fine upstanding man he was — *and* the seed and breed of him, where would you get a better looking fellow or as widely travelled, or as comfortably well off. The evening wore on, they filled their glasses again, and again, Cork poked the fire thoughtfully, scribbled in the ashes and wove his spell until eventually the old man relented. To lose his youngest would be an awful blow to him, Danny was a hard man, and Cork even harder, but if it was Anastasia that Danny wanted then he would have to give in and make the best of it.

'Well I'm delighted' Cork exclaimed, somewhat surprised that the old man had given in at all. 'You know you'll never regret this day, and neither will she! There's nothing left now but to settle the wee matter of a dowry — '

'What!' Big Mick interrupted, jumping up off his chair. 'A dowry! Oh yer a gas man! Where do ye think I'd get money for a dowry? What do you think this is? The Bank of Ireland! That's the last straw, you better go looking elsewhere for a wife and not be takin' up my time! If there's any money to change hands it should be the other way around. You're just after getting the best woman ever a man got and you're still not satisfied. Sure Anastasia's face is her fortune!'

Big Mick's outburst took the two men by surprise, but Cork didn't get his nickname, or his reputation as a matchmaker, for nothing. He was prepared for this scenario; it was all part of the game. He'd been here before!

'That's it. Cork the bottle.' he cried, indicating it was all over.

There had to be a dowry. Reaching for what was left of the *poitín* he stood up and headed for the door:

'C'mon Danny, time to go home, there's going to be no match made here this night.'

Danny was happy enough, he was glad to get her without a penny but Cork shushed him: 'Whisht man, there's a bit of money here, ye'd be as well to take all ye can out of it.'

Cork's bluff worked, Big Mick's bravado disappeared and he backed off immediately: 'Oh, don't get excited, settle down, it's hard on a man having to part with a daughter — and a bagful of money as well'

'It doesn't have to be a bagful, Mick,' Cork replied, turning in his stride, 'but it's the custom and customs shouldn't be either broken or made.'

They sat down again and eventually a dowry of fifty pounds was agreed — on one condition, and Big Mick was adamant: the dowry wasn't going to be paid over until the first child was born. On this he couldn't be moved, so that too was agreed. The men shook hands on the deal; the kettle was put down, more tea made and happy laughter filled the house as plans were laid for the big day.

It was arranged that the three women and the 'Yank' would go into Ballyshannon the following Saturday at three in the afternoon to buy the ring, as well as some other necessities for the wedding.

Well satisfied with his jaunt to Knockbeg Danny and Willie 'Cork the Bottle' McElduff jumped on their bikes and headed off down the road in high good humour. All Danny's plans and dreams were falling into place and he was certain now that coming home was one of the best decisions he had ever made in his life.

Saturday arrived and Danny paced up and down in front of Sheridan's Drapery. It was gone half past three and not a sign of anyone showing up. Had he only dreamed it all or had they talked about it and had a change of heart. Sure who'd have him anyway! Certainly not a fine woman like Anastasia. She was going to have second thoughts and think there was better fish in the sea. The rain beat down on him, trickled down his neck, chilled his bones, dampened his spirits. Anger and despair welled up in him; more than once he darted away impulsively, and then sheepishly retraced his steps. He'd give her another while. Another half an hour went by and his temper flamed again: he was only a fool and sure to be the talk of the countryside. Enough! Turning to hurry away he looked over his shoulder and spotted the three women coming down the street — with Big Mick in tow. Big feckin' Mick! What was he doing here? Who asked him!

Big Mick smiled, Danny glared, the women giggled and they all went into the shop. Not wanting to get involved with women buying their intimate bits and pieces Danny waited uneasily near the exit. Big Mick, not being possessed of sensibilities of any kind, barged in with the women.

Having finished their shopping Danny had a peek at the bill and was shocked when he saw a pair of long johns for the old man along with the other items. Where did that come from! It was customary for the groom to buy a hat for the bride, and one for the bridesmaid. He didn't mind that but it was Anastasia he was marrying, not Big Mick. He wasn't part of the bargain. £26.16.6 the bill amounted to he told the neighbours later. He never forgot it. £26.16.6!

Never mind, perhaps it was a misunderstanding, and though he thought it barefaced cheek on the old man's part he didn't want to seem mean spirited. No point in rocking the boat.

The wedding day arrived and Danny waited anxiously by the altar for the bride. People say there are two days in a man's life that are forever etched in his memory: his wedding day and the day he buys his first house. Most couples facing the walk up the aisle are blissfully unaware that life will never be the same again. No longer will they be masters of their own destiny.

A vision in white lace, his bride-to-be entered the chapel and strolled up the aisle on Big Mick Murtagh's arm. A gossamer veil obscured her face but sure he knew well what vision of loveliness lay beneath. The wedding vows over the pastor, as was customary, invited the groom to kiss the bride. Danny lifted the veil and there to his complete astonishment was the older and plainer, the dark-haired, gap-toothed Priscilla. Afterwards when he told the story to unbelieving listeners and they enquired why he didn't say or do something all he could reply was:

'Well, ye know life isn't perfect, there's always something, if it's not crows its midges and sure I didn't like to make a fuss in front of everyone, I'm thinking she'll do good enough. It could have been worse' he shrugged with a wry grin, 'it could have been Big Mick under the veil.'

With the wedding party over the bride and groom went separately to their own homes that night as was customary. A week later Danny came to collect his bride and her trousseau in a tradition known as the 'drag home'. It was customary also that following the brides moving into her new home she did not visit her parents place for a period of two months. To do otherwise invited bad luck.

They settled in, year followed on long year — each one longer than the last and the bloom went quickly off the rose; hope and prayer went unrewarded, and the deceiver made Danny's life a misery. They had no children and she scolded constantly. No matter how hard he tried Danny couldn't measure up to that giant of a man, the man who could do no wrong, her father Big Mick. Eventually when discussion down at the pub turned to domestic life he wearily referred to his wife as 'The Pill'.

Shortly after the marriage Big Mick arrived one day, found Danny working in the fields, and asked him for the loan of £200.00. A piece of land had come up for sale and he wanted to buy it. He would pay the money back in six months. Danny didn't like the sound of it and he would as soon throw the money into the river as give it to Big Mick but being the soft touch he was, he didn't like to say 'no'. Going into the house after the father had left he asked the 'Pill' what she thought he should do.

'Give him the money', she said. 'Why wouldn't you, isn't he family?

'But what about the dowry? He still hasn't paid that! And now he has the cheek to ask for a loan.'

'What are ye talking about? You know well that the deal was that the dowry would be paid after the first child! Shut up and go out and feed the hens before they eat the bottom out of the door! Yer as lazy as sin.'

Winter turned to Summer turned to Winter again and Danny's cherished hope of offspring wore thinner and thinner. There must have been some periods of truce, the neighbours deduced, because according to Danny it wasn't for the want of trying. He eventually took to drinking and became a frequent visitor to the local pub. Meeting Willie 'Cork the Bottle' one evening Danny bought him a round and they fell into conversation. He listened carefully to Danny's tale of woe and had an answer for him.

'Now it can happen to any man that there won't be family in the house. Have ye tried duck eggs?'

'Duck eggs!' said Danny.

He wasn't sure how to take this advice. Who was supposed to take them: her or him. What were people saying? Was his manhood in question? 'A shut mouth catches no flies' his mother used to advise him. He was giving away too much about his private affairs. But Danny was desperate, the case was a bad one and desperate ills require desperate remedies.

'Duck eggs?' he probed hesitantly.

'Yes,' Willie replied. 'Duck eggs, there's the answer to your problem. There's a cure in them and more strength in them than them oul' hen eggs. If she takes a hardboiled duck egg twice a day or even better still if she takes one raw with a drop of milk fasting in the morning that could be the answer to your problem. Try it for three months and if that doesn't work nothing will!'

Duck eggs were scarce in the countryside, not too many people kept ducks — they weren't as saleable as hen eggs — but that might not be his biggest problem. Even if he could get some how was he going to get the Pill to take them? What excuse could he use? There was no reasoning with the woman. Every time he opened his mouth it started an argument. Still something had to be done. Scouring the countryside for a farm where ducks were reared he eventually found a woman several miles away who had some. She was delighted to find a new customer but, she informed him, the ducks weren't laying right then. He left an order for a regular supply and she assured him that as soon as they started to lay she would send a message.

Danny thought long and hard about how to approach the Pill on the subject. Sometimes it was on the tip of his tongue to say something but time after time his courage failed him. Matters came to a head one evening as they sat by the fireside, she knitting a pair of socks for Big Mick, and Danny, as had become his wont, looking into the fire for inspiration.

'What's the matter with you, you look in a fierce bad humour' the Pill barked suddenly, throwing a savage look across at him. 'Ye have a face on ye'd turn milk sour!'

'Oh nothing at all darling, nothing.... I was just thinking of what my father had to say about a smoking chimney: "If it doesn't draw smoke it'll surely draw tears".

She glared at him.

He paused.

Then taking his courage in his hands:

'I was just thinking about our little problem.' he blurted out suddenly.

'What problem? What are ye talking about,' she said throwing her knitting down. 'If there's a problem anywhere in the world by Jasus you're the man is going to find it!'

Danny backed off quickly as once again his courage failed him.

'What problem are ye talking about?' she said again irritably. 'Speak up!'

'Ah well darling I was just thinking about letting the pasture field out to meadow this year,' he ventured.

'The pasture field out to meadow! Aren't ye lucky has so little to bother you! You know ye should never have left New York at all, not while there's a hole in yer arse will you ever make a farmer!'

Danny blanched under her withering glare and:

'Ah now pet, sure we're not doing that badly, but,' he replied, and despite the danger felt his courage rising a smidge: 'I was just thinking about our other little problem as well' he ventured, casting an uneasy glance across at his nemesis. The cornered animal finds courage.

'Problems, problems, what problems are ye whingeing about now? Spit it out. Suffering Mother of Jasus, what excuse for a man did I marry anyway!'

There was no going back now. No! This was the last chance saloon. There was no other.

'Well you know, love, after all these years we have no children' he quavered.

The Pill's eyes grew wider and wider in disbelief as Danny explained as well as he could what he thought might be the problem. Before he could even get to the duck eggs she exploded.

'Children? Of course we have no children! And whose fault is that? If you were half as good a man as I am a woman the house'd be full of childer! They don't come down the chimney with Santy Claus you know! You're not going to wake up one morning and there'll be a package at the door with a child in it.'

'Well, yes, of course darling, I know that. Maybe we'll make a new start and go on a wee holiday for a while...'

He blundered wildly, blurting out his story about the duck eggs.

'Duck eggs? Duck eggs! Go eat them yourself! If there's anyone here needs duck eggs it's you, there's nothing in the world wrong with me, but I'm afraid it'll take more than duck eggs to put lead in *your* pencil.'

'Ah now Priscilla, don't be like that. I'll tell you what, sure a burnt coal is aisy kindled and maybe we could light the fire again. I'll tell you what; I'll go down and get some of that *magairlín meadhrach* that grows down in the mossy field. They say it's a great tonic and sure it couldn't do any harm. I could do that and sure you might take the eggs. Don't be mad now dear, c'mere and gimme a wee kiss!'

'Kiss! Ye might get something from me, but it's not going to be a kiss! Get outta me way. I'm tired listening to yer nonsense. There's neither ease nor peace in this house with you. I'm goin' to me bed and you!, you can sleep where ye like, don't come anear me this night or I'll not be responsible for what I'll do. Duck eggs indeed!'

Stalking off down to the bedroom, Priscilla left Danny to musing of what might have been had he married Anastasia, the lassie of his dreams? He often thought about her, but there was no going back, he made his bed and now he must lie in it. 'Marry in haste, repent at your leisure'. There was another old saying: 'One lesson bought is as good as two taught' and by God he was paying dear for this one. With a great sigh of relief he thought he had at least managed to bring up the thorny subject of their barrenness. It was the first hurdle negotiated successfully. Even though the conversation didn't go too well he had planted a seed that could grow. Maybe some day soon he could plant that other seed.

Danny's trips to the pub became more frequent and his story became the currency of gossip in Killawaddy. When the ducks eventually began to lay the villagers watched with sly amusement as Danny cycled back and forth. He wore out three bicycles they said. Six months came and went. A year passed by, the ducks stopped laying, started and, as ducks do, stopped again. He cycled back and forth and as he cycled he began to resent more and more his Calvary. The thought of the money that had never been repaid festered increasingly within him as well — but he was too fearful to mention it. Even the matchmaker who suggested he go to the Murtaghs for a woman in the first place regretted giving the advice. He said he never regretted anything as much in his life:

'She's bad company in the neighbourhood,' he said. 'It's the worst match I ever made and it's sorry I am to have walked poor oul' Danny into the hole he's in now.'

Eighteen months came and went and Danny came to accept there would be no children. To add insult to injury neither had the two hundred pounds ever been repaid. He came to hate Big Mick and brooded daily on his misfortune. Plucking up courage he suggested to the 'Pill' that as so much time had gone by they should ask for the dowry. After all he had done his best and it wasn't his fault there wasn't any children. And when was the two hundred pounds to be repaid?

'What are ye talking about?' she snarled at him. 'You have some nerve looking for money back from my father. Didn't ye get me, and isn't that good enough for you?'

And that was the end of that conversation!

Heading for the pub he spent the evening brooding on his misfortune. He had been spending more and more time there lately. As he brooded he drank, and as he drank his resolve hardened. Was he a man or was he a mouse! He was going to face Big Mick. Filled with Dutch courage he mounted his bike and cycled unsteadily out to Murtaghs where he was made as welcome as a rabid dog.

Big Mick peered at him suspiciously: 'What are you doing out here. Ye're drunk again.'

'Well if I'm drunk it's me own money I'm spending. I didn't either borrow it or steal it. Which is more than I can say for some.'

Big Mick's face reddened and he took a threatening step towards Danny: 'What are ye getting at? Go home to your wife!'

'I'll go home when I get me money.'

'And what money might that be?'

'You owe me the two hundred pound you borrowed two years ago — and as well as that you know right well the match was settled with a dowry and I never yet seen a penny of it!'

'The two hundred pounds was a present from my daughter Priscilla. And God help her it was the sorry day she ever set eyes on you! As far as the fortune is concerned you know right well that hasn't to be paid over till the first child is born!'

'Arrah for God's sake would you not give me my money. Haven't I done me best! Haven't I suffered enough. Sure all the soldiers down in Renmore barracks wouldn't put a child in that one.'

Big Mick gave never an inch.

On the way home Danny pondered his dilemma. It was slowly beginning to dawn on him that Big Mick knew all along that his daughter was past childbearing age. He knew right well that he was never going to have to fork over the dowry. The gloss on the green hills of Ireland, that had seemed so attractive to Danny from the Bronx, had faded day by day, year by year. Killawaddy's charms were fast losing their appeal. He had come to hate the farm, the Pill, Big Mike, the small town gossip.

Arriving home the Pill was crouched by the fireside in the attack position — as usual.

'Where were you till this hour of the night?' she barked. 'Out buying drink for the country I suppose and me here on me lone...'

On it went, and on and on, till a savage feeling came over Danny. His fingers curled and he could feel them closing on her throat, silencing forever the shrill voice that, day after day, year after year, had heaped so much abuse on his head. But courage failed him and as he viewed her towering meanness through an alcoholic haze it struck him at last that this is the way it was and, until death do them part, this is the way it was always going to be.

Overwhelmed by a sense of aloneness he put on his hat and gloves and walked out again into the frosty night. Lonely and alone he walked the moonlit strip of road. His senses now sharp as a razor he walked, and as he walked he took it all in, as if for the last time, every sight and sound. A crescent moon hung low in the southwestern sky its bronzed sheen dimly lighting the distant mountains and valleys between. Looking west the Fairy Hill and castle stood boldly silhouetted against a shimmering sea. A sea whose fitful waters whispered and rumbled the secrets of the ages along the ledges and coves of cliff and shore. *Combrá na dtonn*, the conversation of the waves.

Unchanged, the Fairy Hill of his youth loomed memory-laden with secrets of times and people long gone, of his own childhood. Here he had herded his fathers' cattle on the 'long acre'. But what was that he could see now among the rocks, in the quarry face? He stared ever more intently. Mingled with the shadows was that a young boy he could see? Was it a shade perhaps, or a trick of the moonlight? Some wisp of fate or imagination cast away on the hillside? Danny stared dumbfdounded. Was the moon playing some trick on his mind? He seemed to himself not real. Or could it be that the veil between his and the spirit world had slightly parted? Parted to see his youthful self from a time when he kept a lonely vigil here, keeping watch on the family's herd.

His head might burst. Overwhelmed by grief and sadness he broke down and cried, cried salt and bitter tears for the lonely wee boy and for the lonely man. What would he not give to reach out with a kind word or a gift to this phantom? But how could he? A gap of almost forty years separated them. He and destiny's child. A lonely boy had become a lonely man. The man could see the boy but the boy could never see the man.

Was he then a God that stood there watching his younger self? He wished he had never been born. Would it make one bit of difference to anyone if he never had? But he had, and once born would it not be better to fast forward to the inevitable end? The beautiful moonlit waves stretched out before him would take care of that. He could slide under to a peaceful oblivion. His mood deepened. Thoreau had put his finger on it when he said, *'The mass of men lead lives of quiet desperation'*. What are we? Of what are we capable? Are we pre-destined from birth to be failures or successes? Do we really have any control at all over our lives? Are we genetically programmed at conception to be a murderer, a healer, a poet or a drunk? Are our life's paths pre-ordained?

'If you're born to be shot ye'll never be drowned!'.

The moon dipped serenely to the hills cold and aloof from human cares as it looked dispassionately down. So much beauty, and no one to share it with. 'You cannot lie to the moon', a lover once told him. The moon doesn't care. It sees right through your soul. Nothing is hidden. Love is magnified. Sorrow is intensified. Revealed, if only to the moon, is the dark mirror of our loneliness.

Naked we stand.

The image faded into blackness. Lowry the king, on the advice of the Druids, once told his dark secret to a tree. Danny had just shared his desperate loneliness with the spirits of the hills. Putting his mask back on he walked purposefully home by shore and sea. He knew now what he had to do.

Next morning Danny rose early, walked the length of his farm, looked out at the fields he had made so fertile; at the unchanging, indifferent sea, and as he looked his resolve firmed. He loved this land but it wasn't home any more. Home for him now was New York. He missed the never-ending hum of the Great White Way. The freedom and anonymity of the city seemed a greater freedom to him now than the green fields, the country boreens and the squinting windows of Killawaddy. He was gripped by an overpowering urge: he must return. Turning slowly away from the view spread out before him, and fearful to look back in case old ghosts would hold him, he jumped on his bike and headed for Sligo town. There he bought a one-way ticket to New York and freedom.

Spotting Liberty's upraised arm as he flew in over Manhattan Island he felt the warm feeling of old familiar places. Buying a bar on McLean Ave in Yonkers he made more money than he had ever made in construction, or on the farm in Killawaddy. He met and married a Puerto Rican girl who adored him. Settling down to domestic life the years went swiftly by and friends old and new felt at home in 'Barney's Irish Pub'.

His old workmate Muldoon, having heard that Danny was back, made his way to the pub to see him.

'Well Danny, I hate to say I told you so, but that's what happens to most of us who have a longing for home: we finish up back here poorer but wiser.'

Although he would never allow any American to say a bad word about the 'Oul' Sod' it took little prompting to get him to regale Muldoon, or anyone who would listen to him, with stories of Killawaddy and the Pill. When he got to the part about Big Mick and the long johns it brought the house down. That's where he reckoned he should have seen the light: '£26.16.6 the bill amounted to' he never tired of telling his listeners.

Yes, he could never forget it: '£26.16.6, it was the worst investment a man ever made!'

It has often been said that 'you can take the man out of the bog but you can't take the bog out of the man', and although content enough in the new life of his choosing he felt lonesome now and again for home. As he grew older, 'old and grey and full of sleep, and nodding by the fire', his thoughts often turned to Killawaddy's green hills and wave-washed shores.

In every man's secret heart there is a shrine known only to him. In Danny's there dwelt a vision of Anastasia with her soft voice and alluring smile. There he often worshipped while dreaming of the lonely boy on the hillside, of how Love had fled, of Anastasia and what might have been.

# 7

## LAND OF THE FREE

'This is a piece of cake!' Padraig thought to himself as he walked around the floor of the Polycast Technology plant. Wearing a white overall he thought himself quite the cock of the walk and very fortunate to be so well off. He was a quality control inspector no less! One word from him and the company production line came to a halt. America had proven itself to be the Land of Opportunity, the promised land of fame and fortune. Anything was possible here. Quite unlike the home he had left in Ireland, there were no limits to what an honest, hardworking man might achieve.

At home —yes, with all its faults he still thought of it as home — it was not what you knew but who you knew that mattered. If you came from a small farming background as Padraig did, it would be extremely unlikely your family would know anyone of consequence, or at least of consequence enough to pull him into a middling job. His parents, having little education themselves, nor in their time opportunity for it, were wise enough to realise that in it lay the key to a better life.

On small farms sons were prized more than daughters. Their physical strength was more useful in the back-breaking work that was a farmer's lot — and, of no small importance either, they would perpetuate the family name, which girls would not. Regardless of this, Padraig, when he came of age, and although needed to help out on the farm, was sent on to second level education. It was no easy decision and his father while seeing its advantages, saw its disadvantages too. His mother saw only benefit:

'Sure why wouldn't we let Padraig go to the Tech, he's brainy and it would be a shame to let his talent go to loss.'

'Well, it's alright about that, but who's going to do the work? I'm getting on in years and what good is education to a farmer anyway? Experience and the common sense that God gave even to geese is what counts on a farm.'

'Arrah Pat! What are ye talking about? Didn't ye often hear it said that education is no load to carry. If ye want to get on in the world these times you have to have it.'

'Ah, Maggie, Maggie, that's all pie in the sky I tell you. You'll get no good job in this country unless you have pull. And anyway someone has to take over here. I'm not going to live forever!'

'Look Pat! I know you don't mean that. Just because you didn't have an opportunity yourself doesn't mean that Padraig shouldn't. Times have changed and National School just isn't enough anymore. I know what you're thinking but sure can't Padraig take a day off here and there to help when it's time to cut the turf and plant the spuds and so on? Go on, give the lad a chance!'

Knowing he was losing the debate — and anyway his heart wasn't in it — he turned puckish: 'Well didn't you ever hear it said that the dumbest farmer grows the biggest potatoes!'

'Well I never heard such...'

'Ah stop will ye, I'm only coddin', although when I look around me sometimes I think there's a great deal of truth in it. Sure, go on, he'll be a big loss around here but let him go ahead and we'll see what he makes of himself.'

Pat wasn't going to stop his son from acquiring an education, but in doing so was he going to lose him? Was further education the path that would lead Padraig away from home, from his birthright, from everything that mattered? Being a farmer was like having a vocation. There was no great living to be had from it, only plenty of hard work. When the main jobs were done: the crops in, the hay saved, the turf home from the bog, there was the endless chores: cleaning drains, mending fences, thatching the roof: the list was endless — and when the end of the week came or for that matter the end of the month there was no cheque to hand. That would have to wait till the once-a-year crop of calves was sold or the turkeys went to market at Christmas or the all too few creamery cheques that came once a month when the cows were milking in the summertime. It was not a way of life he chose for himself, he just moved into it like one would an old and comfortable overcoat when his father passed on. As natural as the seasons themselves. It was a way of life that passed from generation to generation from so far back that no one could remember who was the first to farm these fields. Nor indeed did anyone ask; enough to know they were there, had always been there and always would be there. Generation after generation of prideful farmers. A 'man of straw' was a man who had no land and therefore no worth, no security, nothing to call his own. There was a great pride in ownership of land!

Husbandry it was called and that's exactly what it was. Husband a farmer was to Mother Earth. He impregnated it not with semen but with seed: grain, potatoes, vegetables, seeds of all kinds. He watched with pride as the Spring rains softly swelled and germinated them, welcomed the sun-filled Summer days that warmed and nurtured. It was inevitable that another generation would follow his to continue that ancient, unbroken link, that spiritual connection.

Padraig was excited and fearful all at the same time. It would be his first venture outside the insularity of his village. He would meet young people from miles around that he had never met before. A strange new world. What would they be like? Would they be mean? Spiteful? Argumentative? Nice? Would he be able to hold his own in this new environment?

'Oh, a shower of bastards!' Sean, who was now in his second year in the Tech, told him as they cycled over on the first morning. This information from someone who should know, having had firsthand experience increased Padraig's fears. A strong wind blew from the South, right in their faces, and they leaned hard on the pedals. Padraig, small for his thirteen years, stood up off the saddle and trod hard to make any progress at all.

'Is that so?' he said breathlessly.

Was it the exertion from cycling, or fear that had his heart thumping so loudly?

'Oh aye', Sean repeated. 'There's a few gorillas from up along the mountain there that'll test you right away.'

That wasn't the news Padraig wanted to hear and he must have looked apprehensive as:

'Ah, there's nothing to worry about,' Sean said reassuringly looking over at him. 'You'll just have to hold your own. Act tough, tell them to "fuck off" right away and they'll know you're not a man to mess with.'

A small knot of noisy newcomers crowded the entrance hall. Raucous though they were, and brash, many must have shared Padraig's fears of their new environment. The quieter ones casually eyed each other up. One lad, bolder than the rest, approached Padraig and:

'Where are you from then?' he enquired.

'Fuck off! said Padraig aggressively, taking the advice given him.

'Oh my!' said the lad, 'there must be some tough men where you come from!'

Padraig didn't have a rejoinder, the lad didn't look hostile, so he decided to be himself and give a civil answer:

'I'm from Killawaddy,' he said.

'Killawaddy? Killawaddy! "The Killawaddy clebs their fingers are wore, pulling the crannach along the shore,"' sniggered the brat.

'That's what you get for being civil,' Padraig thought to himself and before he could think of a smart answer the bell rang and the new arrivals assembled in the classroom.

Their new teacher and principal of the school, Padraig Eamonn Hanrahan swaggered into the classroom carrying a big stick. Sticks were all the rage that time. Padraig was well used to the cane with the nuns in his last school so having had his share of it wasn't intimidated. Facing the class, Master Hanrahan introducing himself in as pompous a manner as befitted a Principal, and a man from Clare to boot, called on each pupil to do likewise.

'Padraig McSweeney,' Padraig answered meekly when his turn came.

'Well? Go on then, where are you from?

' Killawaddy Sir.'

'Ah! It's a great pity those grand old Irish names were ever anglicised. *Tír gan teanga, tír gan anam*! A country without a language is a country without a soul. No wonder you're so small, nothing grows higher than the ditches down by the sea!' he added with a mischievous grin.

'Haw, haw, haw.'

Great gusts of laughter and giggles filled the classroom relieving the tension, at Padraig's expense, of first day nerves for everyone.

'Quiet! What do you think is so funny! This young man bears the name of the great Chiefs of Tír Conall, the Mac Suibhne, descendants of the 4th century High King of Ireland, Niall of the Nine Hostages. A noble line and one of the last to hold out against the English.'

That took the talk off them and they looked at Padraig with a new respect. Things went well from there and in the evening Padraig sped home, this time with the wind on his back, an easy mind and all his fears unfounded. He loved learning and, having got over the first day, looked forward to this new voyage of discovery.

Over the next two years the Master, being full of *tírgráth* himself, instilled in Padraig a love of country and of the countryside. Hanrahan was a rebel at heart and had no time for shoneens, those Irish who admired everything foreign and disdained their own. Much to his father's delight two of the subjects on the curriculum were Botany and Farm Science. He learned about taking soil samples and having convinced his father to have a test done found the soil to be acid. As a result the McSweeneys were the first family to spread ground limestone on the pasture fields. Ten tons of it. Padraig shovelled it on to the ass cart in his free time at weekends and scattered it evenly across the fields.

'Lime and lime without manure makes both the farm and the farmer poor,' was Hanrahan's mantra illustrating the danger of relying exclusively on lime to improve the fields; because of this Padraig and his father spent long hours drawing seaweed from the shore following the Spring storms. This they spread on the now lime-rich fields.

Things were working out very well for Pat McSweeney. His fields grew greener from the new learning employed by his son on the farm. When help was needed Padraig took days off to help with cutting turf and at planting time. Although advances in farming practises intrigued him Padraig's favourite subjects were Metalwork and Mechanical Drawing. At these classes he was taught how to use a T square, set square and drawing board. He learned about oblique and isometric views, isosceles triangles and the square on the hypotenuse. In practical metalworking he learned how to make tools and metal objects using lathes, millers and grinders.

A year went quickly by and, impressed with his performance and fearful that his parents would bring him back to the farm the Principal wrote a letter to them:

*Dear Mr. and Mrs. McSweeney,*

*I wish to inform you that Padraig did very well at his examinations. He excelled in all subjects obtaining honours in Metalworking and Mechanical Drawing. Thus he had 100% success which is excellent. In view of this I thought that if you could spare him & let him continue for another year that he would have a very good chance of the Post Office Engineering Apprenticeship if he continued to show improvement.*

*I know his help is valuable in this adverse harvesting weather but he is young & I think it would be in his own best interests to do another session if you have not alternative plans for him. Also what about his younger brother? We could do with a few more like Padraig.*

*Hoping you are both well,*

*Yours sincerely, P.E. Hanrahan*

Two years of devoted study followed and Padraig, having completed the two year course at the Technical school won his diplomas, again with honours: the *'Teastas do Ghairm-Chúrsa Lae, Lámh - Oiliúnt'* (Manual Training Group Cert) and the Rural Science Group Cert. In conjunction with these he also won the Motor Traders Cert which qualified him for work as a garage mechanic or to be apprenticed to Tool and Die making.

When Padraig decided to apply for work in these fields his father wasn't pleased!

'For God sakes Padraig, what do you want to go looking for a job for when you have a good one here at home?' he asked.

'Dad! I hate to say it but I don't see any future in a small farm.'

'No future? But don't you see yourself how much progress we made since you put what you learned at the Tech into practice. We're already able to keep an extra cow and that's only a beginning.'

'Yes Dad and that's an end to it too. We have only twenty acres, it's stretched as far as it will go and we haven't the money to buy more land, even if it was available — which it isn't!'

'Well go ahead and find out for yourself, but don't come running back here when you find out there's no jobs out there, not unless you have a pull, which you haven't, nor me either. You're your own boss here and you can come and go as you like. You're not tied down by clock or calendar. You plant when the weather is right and reap when the sun shines. Your life is guided by the seasons, not by greedy merchants or petty jealousies —and you don't have to lick anyone's arse for promotion. After the Civil War the farm was run down and I nearly lost my health. I had to go to carpetbagging Blueshirts cap in hand to get a job cleaning drains on the side of the road. It wasn't ability that got me the job, it was whose arse I licked and believe me I wasn't ever very good at that. With all your trigonometry and hypotenuses you'll find it takes more than book learning to get ahead! I never learned about sines and cosines nor did I need to. I know when to plant and when to sow — and when to come in out of the rain!' he finished, breaking into a laugh.

Padraig knew his father had a deep and abiding love of the land and the forces that played on it. He had often seen him in the Springtime of the year, face alight with pleasure, leaning on the gate that led to the tilled fields so ripe with promise; or in the late Summer looking out over the lush green squares studded with haycocks, fruit of the labours of a season's hard work. Puffing his pipe, clouds of blue smoke wafted away into the still air. Noticing his gnarled and calloused hands that gripped the rail Padraig's heart went out to the old man. Poor in pocket but rich in spirit his relationship with these fields was benevolent not exploitative. He gave to the earth and it gave back to him. Spiritually and physically connected he was of the earth, not separate from it, part of a harmonious whole, an integral part of a great plan.

But this was not ever going to be a part of Padraig's plan.

'Well, you know Dad, it doesn't have to be one or the other. As I see it farming is going to be increasingly part time. I could have a job in town and work the farm part time. Farming alone won't provide a living. Increasing mechanisation is on the way. The day of the back-breaking work and the ass or horse and cart is fading fast. Machines will do it faster and more efficiently. You can see already that tractors are coming in...'

'Ah, tractor's, tractors,' Pat interrupted his son, ' that's all I hear about these days is tractors. I'm telling you now that people will regret bringing them in. They're too heavy for the fields around here. And it's not just me saying that! They're bad news for the ground because they compact the soil year after year. It's not natural and won't produce good crops like the horse and plough. We'll see, time will tell.'

'Arrah Dad for goodness sake didn't they say the same thing when people went from the loy and spade to the horse and plough. "Oh, they'll ruin the land, they'll ruin the land, they'll drag the scutchgrass all over the place and choke the crops", was the cry and did they, now tell me, did they?'

'Well Padraig you can't put an old head on young shoulders. When I was your age I thought I knew everything too. Sums can be taught in school, and English and history but life's experience can only be learned by living it. Your own nose will learn you eventually.'

'Is that an okay then Dad? There's plenty of shops and garages in town. I'll go looking to see if I can find work. I have the diplomas to prove that I have the ability and education so it shouldn't take long.'

'If that's what you're bent on doing then go ahead I won't stop you. But the townies are in a class of their own and have little time for the country people, the 'culchies' as they call them. Y'know if the countryman had the arse out of his trousers and the townie the arse out of his, he'd think his arse looked better than the countryman's! It's not so long ago that no business there would employ a Catholic. "No Catholics need apply" was written on the signs they had in the windows when there was a vacancy in a shop.'

'That's all changed now Dad. Martin Harkin down the road there got a job in Henderson's drapery last year. The first Catholic ever to be employed in that shop. That kind of discrimination is a thing of the past, and a good thing it is too! We're all equal now.'

Padraig applied for a job in Harrison's garage. It was the biggest one in town with the most employees. He got to talk to the foreman and was promised that he would be contacted if anything came up. Two weeks went by, and then a month, having heard nothing he decided to cast his net wider. There was something insincere about the foreman's offer anyway he thought. Taking the bus into town twice a week he visited the other garages. When he was done with them he went to the shops. It was the same everywhere he went: either there was no job or he was told that when a job came up he would be contacted. He applied to the County Council, the ESB and P&T. It was no good.

His mother was furious: 'Sure there has to be jobs going. Someone is getting them! That dunce of a Casey fellow down the road. He got a job with the P&T only last week and he hasn't a brain in his head. They must be hard up! How did he manage that? Them Caseys, they're sickeners, tuppence ha'penny looking down on tuppence if ye ask me! It's not so long since they didn't have an arse in their trousers! Why don't you try talking to John Hennigan,' she said addressing her husband, ' he's the County Councillor for this area, maybe he'd do something for Padraig?'

'Ah sure I know Mary, to listen to them, excusing your

presence, you'd think their shite was marmalade! I'm afraid you're barking up the wrong tree there. He's the other side of the house from me and if you don't vote for that crowd, and we don't, they wouldn't give you the smoke off their piss!' his father said ruefully. 'They have enough cronies of their own.'

So that's how it was in this godforsaken country then!' Padraig thought. Yeats had it pinned down it when he said the beggar on horseback lashes the beggar on foot! 'The beggars change places but the lash goes on' he wrote.

*'Hurrah for revolution and more cannon shot;*
*A beggar on horseback lashes a beggar on foot;*
*Hurrah for revolution and cannon come again,*
*The beggars have changed places but the lash goes on...'*

Padraig had relations in America. Maybe he'd go there. To the 'land of the free and the home of the brave.' Yes, that's what he would do. Rise above this petty navel-gazing nepotism. The Irish were on the up and up there. Sure wasn't Kennedy running for President and if he made it, and it looked like he had a good chance, the Irish would be on the pig's back! It was the Land of Plenty and wasn't the parcels they got from their relations there at Christmas proof of that? And the 'American letter' with a cheque in it that was so much prized by his parents. Yes, he would go. His father and mother wouldn't like it but it was time to cut the umbilical cord, time to strike out on his own.

The Americans, as it turned out, were very particular about

who they let into their country. If the 'tired, the poor and the huddled masses' were welcome they had to be financially independent, of a certain standard of education and disease free. Padraig set about making an application for a visa to the American Embassy in Dublin. To get this a letter of recommendation from the Gardai was required to prove there was no criminal record, a medical clearance to show there was no disease or disability and proof of literacy. Evidence had to be produced too that an applicant had enough financial means to support them when they arrived there, or failing that a letter of sponsorship from a relative so that newly arrived immigrants would not be a burden on the American taxpayer.

Having secured his visa Padraig bade a tearful goodbye to his parents. Although devastated with this development they took it in their stride as parents must.

'Good luck son in your new life, son. We're heartbroken to see you leave, but like we always say we won't stand in your way. You'll find that working out there in an unfamiliar world is going to be so much different to working at home. Watch yourself, study hard if you get the chance and remember this advice: if you're working for a company the fellow that's sweeping the floor can be your boss! It's not always brains that gets you ahead.'

Heading for Shannon airport he boarded a plane for New York. In his bag he had a missal given to him as a parting gift from his cousin Sister Mary Brendan, and a letter. He took it out and read it again:

*'Dear Padraig,*

*Please accept this little missal as a memento of your cousin and my visits to your home,'* it read. *'May our Mother Mary keep you under her mantle and may you be a credit to your good parents and to Ireland. Many a young boy has gone to America at your age and with half your brains and have done wonderfully well. You too will do well and surprise us all some day. You'll see and hear things in America but don't be surprised at what you hear. You have had a sheltered life in your happy home. Don't get married too young and I mean that. American boys do marry too young. America is so different to holy Ireland that you need to have a good grip on your faith. Always wear your scapular and carry your beads if possible. Do try to say your daily Rosary and as Fr. Peyton said "All's well!" You'll be in my prayers always.*

*Write home to Mammy and Daddy <u>often</u> won't you and tell them everything. Now goodbye Padraig and God and Mary bless and keep you,*

*Your affectionate cousin in Jesus Christ, Sr. M. Brendan*

Idlewild airport was a swirling, clamouring, maelstrom of teeming humanity rushing hither and thither amidst a deafening racket of carousels, carts, public announcements, baggage handlers and general mayhem. He felt no bigger than an ant in the cavernous building. In at the deep end he thought to himself. Chin up, it's sink or swim now, this is what you looked for, you're where you wanted to be. Make your best of it. He clutched tightly a picture of the aunt that promised to meet him there. In the photo she wore a fur coat and a hat with a feather in it. He scanned the line of people waiting at arrivals and yes, there she was smiling and waving at him. And there was the hat, and the feather! Her kindly face was encouraging: 'Welcome to America', she said throwing her arms around him. 'Welcome, welcome, we're delighted to see you!'

The following days were spent in a dizzy spin of meeting relatives and well-wishers. He felt like a celebrity as his aunts delighted in showing him off, and he was, sort of. There were no Irish where his cousins lived in Westchester County, New York and he might as well have come from Mars. They had never seen a real Irishman before 'right from Ireland' as they said, and neither had they been there themselves. Anything they learned of Ireland came from 'The Quiet Man' with John Wayne and Maureen O'Hara, or 'How are things in Glocca Morra' from 'Finian's Rainbow'. And now here was the real thing, straight from the 'old country'. They showered questions on him and they gave him presents of dollars too. When he had over a hundred dollars gathered together he sent it home to his father and mother. It was the first money he ever had and he felt quite proud that he had money to give them.

Arriving in America is one thing, finding a job is another. At home the very fact that a person went to America was a guarantee of success. But it was no such thing. 'The sidewalks there are paved with gold,' they said. The reality was different and the first thing an emigrant might find out was that the sidewalks were made of concrete! Secondly many of them weren't paved at all, but third and most important there was money to be had from paving them. Sure there were fortunes to be had in the New Land. But it was acquired from hard graft, business acumen, perseverance, long hours and more than a bit of luck. Land of Opportunity it was, but opportunities must be recognised for what they were, and grasped

'Padraig! There's a few days work going on a building site. I know the boss and I can bring you down in the morning! Will you take it?'

Would he take it? Well, would a cat drink milk? It wasn't what he wanted but sure maybe that would come with time. This was a bird in the hand and a beginning, albeit a modest one.

The boss, a Jan Frederici, (they had very strange names in this country!) was waiting for Padraig when his cousin brought him to work in the morning. Right away he was given a wheelbarrow and instructions to clean up the ground in preparation for landscaping. Frederici's wife came too and the three of them stood watching Padraig with benevolent expressions on his very first job in America.

Well used to hard labour Padraig set to work immediately loading the barrow with rocks and stones. Wanting to give a good impression to the watchers he filled the barrow to the brim, and more. Grasping the handles he set off down the site — and suddenly it all came apart for him. Bouncing off a small stone the wheel buckled under the impact, and as if that wasn't bad enough, in capsizing, the handles gave Padraig a clout on the side of the head knocking him sideways. He was mortified and his face blazed with embarrassment. It wouldn't be so bad if no one was watching but what kind of a first impression was this to give? Things couldn't get any worse — they could only improve.

And they did.

Scanning the 'help wanted' advertisements in the newspaper he took anything he could get till he found employment in a factory in Ossining, New York. His diploma the *'Teastas do Ghairm-Chúrsa Lae, Lámh - Oiliúnt'* earned before he left home, created great merriment and everyone in the shop gathered round to see this strange testament. It might have been one of the Dead Sea scrolls for the interest it aroused. It's the 'Manual Training Group Cert' he explained to them with a great deal of embarrassment. With a little bit of bluff, his diplomas, and more than a bit of padding on his work experience, which up to then had been only turfspades and wheelbarrows, he was given a job in the machine shop.

What he lacked in learning he made up for in enthusiasm and hard work. Not just that, but he made friends as well who helped him out when he was given a job too complex for his limited experience. Having as always a voracious appetite for learning he went to night classes. There was no such opportunity at home so he just couldn't believe his luck and couldn't get enough of it! Taking advanced Blueprint Reading and Machine Shop he expanded the skills he had learned in his school days.

Twelve months in the job he felt that, although he had gained a lot in skill and experience, his opportunities for promotion in this small company were limited. Looking for advancement he saw an advertisement by Polycast Technology in Portchester, N.Y. to fill a vacancy as a quality control inspector. A quality control inspector! Well that would be a big jump. But then again he pondered, how hard could it be to inspect other people's work? Building up his confidence with the thought: 'Nothing ventured, nothing gained!' he went for the interview.

As luck would have it the Quality Control manager, Terry Nugent, was Irish American. Tall and lanky with a shrewd, enquiring countenance thatched with bushy eyebrows that moved like caterpillars he picked up instantly on Padraig's accent:

'What part of the old country are you from?, he asked.

'Sligo,' Padraig answered.

'Are you long here? How do you like it'

'Over a year now. I like it well enough.'

'My father is from Sligo and my mother from Leitrim. What took you over here?'

'There was very little work at home and what work there was if you didn't have a pull you hadn't a chance,' Padraig told him.

'Well, this is the country for you then! Can you read a calipers and micrometer?' he queried.

Can I read a micrometer! Padraig thought. Can I read a micrometer? Sure if you knew anything at all you would know that.

'Yes sir, I can.'

'What machines did you work on in your last job?'

'Engine lathe, Bridgeport miller and surface grinder mostly.'

'Come on with me, I'll show you around the place. Can you start on Monday?'

'Well, I'd like to give a weeks' notice where I'm working now but I can start the following Monday.'

Padraig was euphoric on the way home. Well, that was easy enough, he thought! He had not just got the job, but hit on luck finding what was practically a fellow Irishman in this position of responsibility. He was amazed at how many Americans he had met that had an Irish background or an Irish aunt or uncle hidden somewhere in the closet. All his hard work and night school had paid off and now he felt he couldn't put a foot wrong. He was going to make a lot more money than in the last place and with a fellow Irishman as boss he felt he had the inside track right away. This was indeed the land of equal opportunity. You were measured here by what you could do, not the small-minded, parochial *who* you were of home!

Nugent showed him the ropes, what he had to do, what mistakes might be made in the machine shop and how essential it was to catch them before prototypes went into production. These were component parts for the new Boeing 727 airplane. People's lives depended on them working properly. It was challenging work and more responsibility than he ever had before. He couldn't get any job at all at home and now here he was in his white coat, cock of the walk!

A long way indeed from Killawaddy to Portchester!

Being a young and developing company new employees were brought in from time to time. Glad to see the company growing Padraig noticed with interest as the months went by that new people were coming into his department. He was quietly pleased to see that they were not up to his level of skill or knowledge. He was astonished to see that of the three employees taken on one of them couldn't even read a micrometer! Another one couldn't make heads or tails of a blueprint. Not that he took any pleasure at their ignorance of the basics but it just might mean if there was promotion any time in the future he would be well qualified.

As he became increasingly familiar with the details of the job he could sometimes spot more efficient ways of inspecting the product, and when he did he brought these to the attention of his boss. He even spotted small changes that could be made to make the production line run smoother and ideas for patents on new products. What was good for the company, he reasoned, was good for his boss and what was good for his boss had to be good for him too. Nugent listening to his suggestions sometimes made changes and sometimes not. Sometimes he seemed to have trouble understanding the underlying mechanics of Padraig's suggestions. In hindsight Padraig reflected afterwards that Nugent did not always seem pleased at his suggestions and he was at a loss to understand why. Was it his imagination or did his boss actually resent Padraig's suggestions! But of course not, it had to be wild imagining. Padraig dismissed the thought completely and continued his work with unabated enthusiasm.

'Padraig! Can you come into the office for a minute, I have an announcement to make?'

The invitation came first thing on a Monday morning. Padraig wasn't surprised. He had been with the company a year and a half now. Their section had been very busy of late and he ventured to think that a promotion might be on offer. Nugent had been overwhelmed with work and it was obvious that he needed assistance. Assistance! That would mean then that there might be a job opening for an assistant manager. Dare he hope against hope that having seniority and a very good grasp of his work the job might be offered to him? He got on well with his boss and workmates and that too would surely be taken into account when a decision was being made.

When he entered the office all the staff of the quality control department were there.

'Gentlemen! I called you all together this morning as I have an announcement to make.' Terry Nugent began.

'As you all know this company is expanding exponentially. As a result our department is also getting bigger and bigger. The reason for the success of Polycast Technology is that our product is top rate. And the reason our product is top rate, if I may say so, is the achievement of this Department in spotting defects and flaws before they go to the mass production. My suggestions re improvements on the production line and efficiency in inspecting the various products has not gone unnoticed by management'

Padraig listened attentively. This was all music to his ears and he took a great pride in being part of the success of this, his company, his team. No matter that Nugent was taking credit for his suggestions re efficiency. Teamwork! That's what it was: one for all and all for one.

'Following a meeting with the Board of Directors it was decided that I should select an assistant. Having considered the matter very carefully the assistant I have chosen, I am very pleased to tell you this morning, is Bob Moffat...'

Padraig was stunned! The rest of Nugent's announcement was just a blur of words. He couldn't take it in. Bob Moffat! The man that couldn't even read the basic inspection instruments, that was always dodging work, hanging the dog going to Nugent's office on every pretext.

Swallowing his disappointment he congratulated his workmate. Life goes on. After all why should he be disappointed? He was getting paid for his work. There never was any promise or guarantee of promotion. There would be another chance, he wasn't going to let this put him off his stride. Returning to his work with renewed zeal he quickly forgot his frustration.

The company continued to expand and in time another chance did come — and again it was another workmate that was promoted. Padraig was shattered. How could this be? Why was he getting passed over every time? Shades of his experiences at home! 'The more things change the more they stay the same,' he thought.

Then, in a Damascene moment of revelation it occurred to him: Was he *too* good for his job? Could it be that the only people Nugent wanted close to him were those who were no threat to his position, whose technical expertise was much less than his? In wanting to be helpful had he inadvertently revealed to his boss that he was much more competent than him? Padraig punched his time clock that evening for the last time. Yes, he had made up his mind. He would not, could not, go back.

The newfound gods of his Promised Land, it turned out after all, had only feet of clay. He walked out into the evening sunshine and after a while he shrugged, smiled and laughed: he was free, free to begin again. 'One lesson bought is as good as two taught,' he had heard his mother say, and this was not the first nor would it be the last, of the many lessons he would learn. A great load was lifted off him.

Homeward bound he heard music in the evening rush hour traffic and saw hope in the golden rays of the setting sun.

# 8

## THE STOLEN CHILD

*'Away with us he's going,*
*The solemn eyed:*
*He'll hear no more the lowing*
*Of the calves on the warm hillside*
*Or the kettle on the hob*
*Sing peace into his breast,*
*Or see the brown mice bob*
*Round and round the oatmeal-chest.'* [8]

Northwesterlies had swept the fields and stone ditches of Inishmurray for weeks, flattened the grass, sent billows thundering between the high cliffs of *Poll a Seantoinne*, clawed vainly at the frail fishing craft drawn high up on the shore. There were no trees or hedges for shelter. The salt-laden wind that blew almost constantly over the land saw to that. Wise ancestors had chosen the sheltered eastern shore — away from the prevailing westerlies and facing the rising sun — to build a stretch of houses from *Baile Thiar* (West Village) to *Baile Thoir* (East Village).

These houses, generally a kitchen with a bedroom on either side, provided shelter and comfort for a population of around

8  *The Stolen Child*, W.B. Yeats

a hundred souls. A brace and hearth fire, taking up most of one wall, dominated the kitchen. Built into the opposite wall of the kitchen, down beside the door, was a dresser displaying the family china, beside that a stone shelf for a water vessel and above it a wooden rack where dried fish were hung. Standing around on the stone-flagged floor and blackened with use and age were the three-legged cast iron pots, ovens and pans used in cooking for cattle, poultry and family.

Snugly on one side of the fireplace was a 'hag' or 'pooch' bed built into the wall. This bed, warm and comfortable, was generally reserved for the older members of the household: grandparents or parents  More than just a kitchen this room was the life and hearts blood of the family — and of the community. Around it, generation followed generation; life unfolded, blossomed and passed on: children grew into adults, adults into old age. There in the hag bed beside the fire children were born; when death called this is where the old people were waked. When neighbours gathered in at night, time told by clock or calendar became irrelevant. Around the crackling flames, within the semicircle of light, the impossible became possible; past and present merged in a homogenous bygone. It was no matter. Enough to know it happened. Chronology was immaterial and all thoughts connected only to emotion and place.

No boat had put to sea since the storm began; rations were running low and the islander's plight desperate. Now, in Dominick 'Crimley' Harte's house, with the wind booming in the chimney and the door battered by driven rain, concerns of the storm outside and empty shelves were put aside for a while.

'It was in weather like this long ago that the good people, the *daoine sidhe* came to steal a child from the islanders,' Crimley declared, looking into the heart of the fire.

The dancing flames and spiralling smoke stirred the imagination of narrator and listener alike; storytellers like Crimley drew from its heart's core as from a bank. A living treasury of the mind unrecorded in any book. Young storytellers there were none, for they lacked the patina of wisdom and knowledge that came only with age.

'There's things happened long ago that ye'd never hear about anymore,' he continued, and ye know this island is still an enchanted land. The fairies have their place and it's a brave man, even now, that'd make a throw of whiskey without giving the first drop to the *daoine mhaith*, the good people of the island. Before the Angelus bell was heard here this place was very gentle[9].'

It was St. Molaise that brought the Christian bell to Inishmurray when he established a monastic settlement there in the 6th century. Before that the allegiance of those who lived there was to the hidden people of the old religions. When Oisín of the Fianna met St. Patrick he heard the Christian bell for the first time. Unimpressed he told Patrick that when his leader Fionn and the Fianna lived they much preferred to be listening to the whistle of the blackbird: 'the voice of the bells would not have been sweet to them.' And so it was on Inishmurray, those old gods were remembered with affection, they that held the allegiance of the Irish before the Angelus bell was heard.

9 Under the influence of the fairies

Not that they would have been consciously perceived as such but gods they were, their unwritten beliefs and taboos long held in esteem alongside the more fundamental teachings of Christianity.

'And mentioning whiskey,' Crimley went on, asking the question that was heavy on everyone's mind, 'what are we going to do at all? The island is awash with it. The people out in Cloonagh and Killawaddy are crying out for it and no way of getting it to them. They must think we're dead — and if this storm doesn't lift soon I'm afraid we will be. There's not a loaf left on the island and if we don't shortly get a boat out to the mainland we'll be penniless — and starved! We might have to try 'Colmcille's Path.'

Their situation was worrying and their concern well grounded. When the first gusts blew, the boats were pulled up on to high ground. Now with the sea still in a frenzy, the spume from *Lochán* swirling about their houses, and the wind tearing at the thatch, no craft, big or small, dare venture out of Clashymore harbour. It was a belief that any boat that ever sailed on the path that St. Colmcille once took to get to Inishmurray would never go down. Many hundreds of years ago, on one of Colmcille's visits to his confessor, St. Molaise, the boatman didn't show up. Not to be deterred the holy man raised his hand, 'the sod opened before him', and he walked to the island. But who was going to put that to the test now? Faith has its limits!

Flour had run out completely. There were only potatoes left and no meat. This caused the women to have resort to their few non-laying hens for dinner, and their stock of dried fish: mackerel, pollock, cod and ling, that had been salted last Autumn and had to last them for the rest of the winter.

'Ah whisht man', Sean O'Baoil growled at him. 'Ye'd think listening to ye this was the first storm ever blew. We've come through worse. You're always talking about Colmcille's Path but that's as far as it gets: talk! We'll send someone out to *Tobar na Cabhrach* in the morning. It's safer.'

He paused and: 'Me father, God be good to him, used to say: "We never died a winter yet, and the divil wouldn't kill us in the summer!"' he said laughing as he tried to lighten the conversation and the seriousness of their dilemma.

*Tobar na Cabhrach* (the Well of Assistance) was one of the many stations dotted around the perimeter of the island that had been established during its monastic era. When the islanders were in distress, say a doctor or priest urgently required or food supplies exhausted, the waters of the well calmed the sea. The procedure was to walk around the well three times, and while doing so to throw three cupfuls of the water against the wind, in the name of the Father, Son and Holy Ghost. A practise that pre-dated the Christian era and the appeal made in ages past to the old Celtic gods of the island!

Some scoffed at these beliefs and said it was a load of old pistroges; that any time the procedure worked it was co-incidence and the storm would have abated anyway. More firmly believed in the practice: How could the belief have survived all those years if there wasn't truth in it? The old people did it long before their time and any number of instances could be cited to prove the miraculous powers of the well.

Next day Crimley and Sean made their way to the well to perform the ritual: 'Have tomorrow calm or we'll be hungry,' they said as they prayed.

Miracle or coincidence, the following morning when the islanders awoke the storm was gone. In place of the clamour of wind and ocean a strange stillness had descended. Day after day for weeks, and higher than a house, the breakers had come roaring in on the reefs of *Bolg Bán* and *Banc Rue*. The roar of thunder from *Poll a Seantoinne*, the chasm of the mighty wave, was loud in their ears all day and all night. It filled their waking as well as their sleeping hours. Now there was a silence so quiet that it almost seemed loud, unnatural.

When they talked about it afterwards the islanders were all in agreement that something strange was afoot that morning. Not a breath of air stirred; a heavy mist hung on the sea; familiar objects, half hidden by wraiths of vapour swirling on the still water, looked strange and unfamiliar. No bird sang; the cock's crow that was always heard didn't break this perverted silence. It never happened before. The very air was heavy with portent. It should not have been ignored. Only a fool would go about their day's work or set foot on fair or market till the cock crew. Everyone knew that. The cock's dawn crow banished the spirits of the dark. Across the water on the Maugherow peninsula no one lifted a finger till the cock gave his haughty summons. He was a reliable clock too, of which there were few on mainland or island.

It seemed that the very laws of Nature were suspended, upended on that fateful morning; the natural rhythm of island life thrown into chaos.

It started when Sean O'Baoil was startled into wakefulness by a loud rapping on the windowpane. Jumping out of bed he pulled the curtain back and there on the street and full of excitement was an old fisherman from *Baile Thiar*. Sean was surprised to see him as the man had long given up the calling on account of rheumatism and numerous crippling joint pains brought about by repeated wettings, hard days and cold nights — the curse of those that earned a living from the sea.

'Get down as quick as you can to Clossy,' he shouted to Sean. The sea is settled and our famine is over. There's an awful glut of fish there, the biggest I ever seen.'

Sean looked sleepily around him. It was bright day and he had slept in. The realisation slowly dawned on him that he hadn't heard the cock crowing; if he had he wouldn't have still been in bed. The old man hopping about with excitement kept on about the great glut of fish and to get over there right away.

'It's not right to be out', says Sean, 'till the cock crows.'

'Oh, cock here or cock there,' says the man, 'this load of fish isn't going to stay there forever. They're there in heaps in the Clossy now.'

'I don't know' Sean hedged, 'it's not right. No good will come of it!'

'Oh never mind them old pistroges! Aren't we starving here for the last three weeks with the dint of storm! What's wrong with ye? Go down right away and get as many fish as you can. Take some of them to sell to the mainland — and a few kegs of *poitín* as well. There's enough fish down there to feed everyone on the island and half the mainland as well. God blast that oul' cock. If I get near him I'll take the head off him. He'll make better soup than timekeeper. Damn pistroges! Go on! Go! If I was in better shape I'd be down there myself already and not be depending on the likes of ye!'

Much against his better judgement Sean harnessed his two donkeys with creels and straddle and headed over to Clossy. When he got there the air was alive with wings and a deafening clamour of seabirds: blackbacks, common gulls, terns, kittiwakes, gannets; it seemed that every creature that flew had gathered there to feast.

Forgetting his concerns Sean got caught up in the excitement and joined the other islanders in the melee. Drawing their nets across the inlet they hauled bagful after bagful of fish up on to the rocks: pollack, herring and glassin. The likes had never been seen on the island before. When the boxes overflowed they piled the fish up on the rocks till they had what looked like three or four ton of fish piled high.

On his way over the boreen with two ass loads of herring Sean O'Baoil noticed that the cock still hadn't crowed, and thought to himself how unnatural a thing it was to be out fishing at all. But food was food, he reasoned, and this was an opportunity that couldn't be missed. Blessing himself with the sign of the cross he went on and decided to drop the first load of fish into a house where there lived an old woman, Biddy Mc Gowan, with her daughter Mary and a babe in arms.

'God save all here,' Sean said as he pushed in the door. The old grandmother was up but the daughter and child were still in the pooch bed.

'Arrah, musha is it yourself is in it.' the old woman said. 'Come in, come in, and welcome. What time of the day is it at all?'

'Oh it's a quare time of day to tell you the truth. We're wore out all morning with the dint of killing fish down in the harbour. I'll throw this lok down in the room for ye if ye like. There's plenty for everyone'

'Oh God bless ye Sean but it's you has the good heart. We put in an awful time this past few weeks with storm and want. That poor girl there has hardly enough milk in her breast to feed the child.'

Sean threw the creels of fish on an old sail cloth on the floor of the lower room. When he was done the women thanked him profusely. The old woman started to kindle the fire in preparation for cooking the windfall and Sean headed back down to Clossymore to draw the rest of the fish.

He was no longer out of the house than the door burst open and in through the kitchen came a big black and white sow. Bigger than anything they had ever seen before. Heading straight for the fish it ate and rummaged and scattered them all over the floor. The young woman screamed and jumped out of bed to help her mother hunt the pig out of the house. The child taking fright at all the commotion started to cry. They tried to shoo it out the door but it turned on the two women. Grunting and biting it chased them out of the room. What with the child crying, the young woman shouting and the pig grunting savagely the kitchen became a battleground. Thoroughly frightened now, the old woman took an ash plant and the young woman the tongs and went back to face the beast. Struggling fiercely they managed to beat it out the door. Back in the house again they looked at each other mystified as to where the pig came from.

'Where in the name of God did that brute come from, Mary? Did you ever see it before?'

'No Mammy, it must have broke out of some house where it was kept. And the colour! Black and white, I never saw the likes before. There's no one on the island has a black and white pig that I know of.'

The child was still whimpering so Mary climbed back into bed beside him. The old woman had kindled the fire and was pulling out hot coals on which to put the frying pan when the door burst open again and in came the pig and straight down to the room where the fish were stacked. Biddy straightened up from the fire and turned around, astonishment written all over her face. Mary looked at the pig and then at her mother her face as white as a sheet.

'Mother of Christ', the old woman exploded letting let out a string of curses as she made for the iron tongs again while damning the strange pig into hell and out again:

'C'mon Mary, gimme a hand? This damn pig'll not get the better of us!'

Confronting the strange beast again the old woman battered it with the tongs and the young woman with a heavy wooden 'beetle' normally used for pounding the big iron pots of spuds. Scales and mashed fish were spattered all over the floor and walls in the fierce struggle. The pig charged Biddy knocking her into the middle of the fish but Mary hit it a mighty whack drawing it off the older woman. By now the women's dresses were a mess of gore and fish scales but they fought on determinedly until they succeeded in chasing it out of the house and down the grassy road. This time they kept chasing it until it ran off across the fields and out of sight.

The women spotted Sean O'Baoil in the distance on his way back from Clossy with another load of fish. Running up to him screaming and crying and: 'Come over quick,' they shouted, "there's something unnatural came into the house'.

'What's up? What's wrong?'

They told Sean about the strange pig, the colour of it, the attack it made on them and about it coming back into the house a second time. As they talked they heard a faint crying in the air; a plaintive wail that seemed to emanate from *Baile Thoir* travelling in the direction of *Caiseal*. It was a rushing, soundless, yet powerful noise. Strange and at the same time familiar. What in God's name could it be? No! No! Biddy had never heard anything like it before and her heart froze. Or did she only imagine it? With so many strange things going on that morning it might be nothing more than a combination of fatigue, hunger and an excited imagination.

Says Sean: 'Is there anyone in the house with the child?'

'No, we left him in the kitchen bed when we chased the pig away up the fields.'

'Ye chased it away up the fields and left the child in the house on its own? Did ye put the tongs across the cradle before ye left?'

'No we didn't, we forgot, we were frightened out of our lives that the beast'd kill us within in the house!'

'I'm afraid it's a bad thing ye did to leave the child on its own. The iron has power over the unnatural, fairies or such that might want to steal the child. No island woman ever left a child in the house to go for water to the well or anywhere without putting the tongs across the cradle. You should know that! C'mon now, we better get back as quick as we can,' said Sean leaving the ass and creels and hurrying with the women over the boreen to the house.

When they got there they were relieved to see the child still safe in the pooch bed. It was crying and squealing hysterically but they didn't mind, they were just glad to see it was alright..

Greatly relieved Mary picked up the baby hushing it and soothing it and putting it to her breast. To her great surprise, instead of taking the milk the infant snarled and bit her nipple. Crying out with pain she immediately dropped it into the cradle where it continued to wail and scream.

Surprise written all over their faces the two women and Sean looked at each other in dismay. What was going on here? This was quite out of character for their child. Had their worst nightmare come to pass? Was Sean right? Was the child they had left behind now with the fairies in *Caiseal* and this creature, this changeling, this *sídheog*, left in its place? The baby they had known was a placid child, good humoured and a pleasure to feed, bathe and nurture. How could it be that a baby's personality could change so completely and so suddenly? Could it be that the incident with the pig was nothing more than a diversion to lure the women away from the house. They reluctantly came to the conclusion that it was indeed a changeling and that it was not their child that bit the nipple of the breast of the mother.

The women were distraught:

'Sean! What are we going to do at all? What can we do?'

'The best thing you can do is go for Dominick Harte. There's nothing he doesn't know about things like this. He'll soon tell you whether it's a changeling or not — and if it turns out that it is he'll know what to do about it.'

Greatly assured the women sent for Dominick who was down fishing at Clossy with the other men. He shortly arrived with a gaggle of neighbours in tow. Word had spread about the island and everyone was curious to see the child that all the commotion was about.

Greatly respected by the islanders a silence fell on the gathering when Dominick walked into the kitchen. Having no doctor stationed on the island he was the medicine man that people went to when they were sick or injured. He held the secret of all the old remedies that had been handed down for thousands of years: cures for burns, fractures, pain in the head, heart fever. Whether it be a paste, potion or laying on of hands Dominick had the power and the secret recipes, prayers and incantations that seldom failed. There was nothing he couldn't cure.

Walking slowly up to the cradle he looked in at the child. It looked back at him wild eyed and it yelling an' squealing away at the top of its voice.

Holding the child's gaze: 'Someone get me a sheaf of straw',

Dominick said quietly. 'We'll soon see about this *ceolán* in the cradle!'

'Ye're not a right thing', says Dominick addressing the child when he was handed the sheaf, 'the natural child,' says he gravely, 'was taken. The pig that came into the house was in a disguise, it was in a disguise, but we know now it was wan of your fairy people, an' the child was taken an' brought over to the *Caiseal*.'

At that the *sídheog* in the cradle stared hard at Dominick as if it was trying to figure him out or what his intentions were. It quit yelling.

'An' now," says Dominick his voice rising to a shout, "I'm going to burn ye within in the cradle".

The little gathering drew back with a gasp fearful of what would happen next. One swift movement and Dominick had grasped the sheaf of straw, went over to the fire, lit it and turning smartly bounded towards the cradle. In an instant the child leaped out on the floor, ran out the door like a flash and away across the field until it was out of sight. For days and weeks afterward the island was searched from shore to shore but the real child never was found, nor did it ever return! No trace of either the *sídheog* that was in the cradle, or the child that was taken, ever was seen again.

༺

As the years wore on the story became a legend. It was told and re-told and eventually a younger generation doubted that such a thing could ever happen. Sometimes they would ask Cáit McGowan if it could be true.

'Did that really happen?' they would say

'Oh, *agradh*", she would answer,' 'be the virtue of my oath *asthore*, me sister was taken away with the good people of the island. An' to this day I'm warning every woman that has a young child on the island, never leave the house after dusk. If they go out for water down to the well or go visiting a neighbour's house; before they leave, if there's a child in the cradle, a young child, always take the tongs from the hob or the hob corner an' put the tongs across the cradle. 'Twas done with all the childer of the island. When you have the tongs across the cradle the good people has no power over that child, they can't take that young person away.'

From that day forward no child was ever again left without a tongs on the cradle — and never again was the black pig seen, or a child ever stolen.

# 9

## WHERE THE GOOD MEN IS

Barney Wilson had lately come into a bit of money and bought himself a 1940 Ford Coupe. It was ten years old but in good nick with small mileage — or so the previous owner claimed. Barney, spotting an opportunity, started right away into the hackney business. Endless possibilities beckoned. He would no longer have to confine his escapades in pursuit of *l'amour* to the parish boundaries, and neither would his acquaintances. He wouldn't forget them, and he was certain they would be glad to pay him some small sum for the convenience of being carried in style to rendezvous near and far.

Petrol rationing was still in force so Barney had to lay his plans carefully. Coupons as well as cash had to be produced for every gallon purchased. Difficult choices had often to be made: a trip to the bog or a trip to the dancehall. The 'Rules of the Road' had not yet been written; there was no limit to the number of people that could be carried and even if there was, it wasn't enforced. From the punters point of view the more passengers that could be packed into a car the more affordable the fare. Barney's proud boast was that he could 'carry a football team' when he was put to it. No space was wasted. Even the boot held two men.

The beauties that lived in the village had high notions Barney's friends all agreed; they wouldn't give the time of day to the local lads — and he considered it no big loss for they had exaggerated notions of their charms. And anyway you couldn't chance one of them even if you wanted to. It wasn't worth the risk of being turned down by a damsel that you met every day. You'd never live it down! Now he and his friends could spread their net to faraway places: beyond the mountains to Glenfarne maybe, or even further afield to that shining palace of dreams, the Silver Slipper Ballroom in Strandhill. There they would meet exotic creatures, maybe even themselves seem exotic to new eyes in faraway places.

Propositions came in all forms. This one came on a Sunday after Mass outside the chapel gates where the men of the village gathered to discuss news of the week gone by, weather prospects for the week ahead, price of cattle and all matters of such vital importance to the inhabitants of Killawaddy.

Mickey Joe Higgins and two more of the village playboys broke free of the older men and went over to Barney who was leaning with studied nonchalance against his new chariot. Barney was an easy-going sort of fellow, short and fat with a ruddy, smiling face and bushy eyebrows capped by a shiny pate where once a full crop of hair bloomed. He was extremely conscious of the lack and had watched with dismay as day by day his locks became fewer and fewer. Once, when there was still hope the decline could be arrested he took the advice of a well-intentioned neighbour and shaved his head in the belief it would re-invigorate growth. Contrarily, it never grew again!

'Aloysius here wants to get up to Collooney but he doesn't want to get back. We'll pay ye the full fare though, he says there's a dance there tonight,' said Mickey Joe acting as spokesman.

'What's wrong with Aloysius? Can't he talk for himself!'

Barney was immediately suspicious as Aloysius had a reputation for being 'as tight as a crab's arse' and maybe he was looking to cadge a free ride. A slippery character that kept his cards close to his chest: that was Aloysius. And why was Mickey Joe speaking up for him? That was a surprise! The two were well known to be rivals in nearly everything from who could grow the biggest praties to who could land the best looking woman on a night out.

'Never mind that, we want to go, can ye take us or not?'

'Have ye enough to make a load?'

'No! There's only three of us in it, but sure it'll take us no time to get a few more together!'

'Alright then, be down at the corner of Guckian's Hotel tonight at eight o'clock and we'll see,' Barney was cautious still, but at the same time delighted with the prospect of making a bit of money and, as a bonus, having a night out for himself as well.

Guckian's was a two storey slated pub cum hotel and it was at the gable end of this establishment that the local corner boys gathered in the evenings when the wind blew from the east. Not indeed that they were all 'corner boys' which was a derogatory label, but 'tell me your company and I'll tell ye what y'are' fathers warned their sons. Which wasn't very fair when you think about it because it wasn't like there was that much choice of places to go — and in any case corner boys were always more interesting company than altar boys! When the wind changed and blew from the west they moved across the road to Moffit's gable. East wind or west wind they never had enough money to go inside and bask in the comfort of Guckian's snug with a frothy pint to their lips.

By eight o'clock Mickey Joe had gathered enough of a crew to make the trip, eight in all. They waited anxiously at the appointed venue. Barney, half an hour late as usual, pulled up in a cloud of dust and crunching of gears — he still hadn't mastered complete control of his new conveyance — and, giving them a critical look, declared:

'Jasus lads, don't ye know it's to a dance ye're going, not to the bloody bog.'

Conscious of the pristine condition of the interior of his newly acquired and cherished acquisition he went on:

'Could ye not clean yourselves up a bit better? Ye'll never get a woman lookin' like that!'

'Kettle calling black arse to the pot,' Mickey Joe responded spiritedly. Thinking himself to be the 'bees knees' he was stung by the criticism.

'What do you care? Yer getting paid aren't ye! What more do ye want! And what in hell kept you so long anyway we're perished here waiting!'

Mickey Joe was the perennial bachelor: a small farmer of fifty, going on sixty summers that lived at home with his father and still hadn't given up the chase. Deep in the recesses of his mind, as with many a bachelor, was a glimmer of hope that never quite extinguished. Their stone built, whitewashed cottage was typical of the time: thatched, kitchen in the middle with a room at either end. The old man, white whiskered and bent, slept in the warm 'hag bed' in the kitchen while Mickey snored the night away in the lower room.

Indeed and it wasn't Mickey's fault to be on the shelf the local fishwives allowed when he came in their sights. His father was a contrary old man with lean jaws and wicked eyes that impaled Mickey on his every peccadillo. Like most men Mickey felt the urge of the paternal instinct, although to him this call was indistinguishable from a strong desire to mount any willing female. His impulses were effectually curbed, not alone by his disapproving father, but by the rigid codes enforced by any number of priests of the Catholic Church; priests that gave vent to their disapproval of any liaison that wasn't sanctified at the altar.

*'...And Priests in black gowns, were walking their rounds, And binding with briars, my joys and desires.'*[10]

Bowing to these conventions Mickey had, years before, introduced Maggie Kate, a woman that he had a strong notion of, to his father. The old man, immediately seeing her as a threat, was not to be displaced now or ever, and:

'What are ye bringing that prostitute in here for?' he demanded.

'What are ye talking about Daddy? She's not a prostitute!'

10   *The Garden of Love*, William Blake

'Well, look at ye! Who else'd have anything to do with you.' the old man stabbed.

Mickey Joe would not be discouraged however. Making a cup of tea for Maggie Jane he tried his best to make pleasant conversation.

'Sure ye know her people Daddy. They come from the townland of Cloonabawn. Her father has a big farm there.'

The old man knew all about Cloonabawn, a barren bogland that wouldn't feed a snipe. It was too far away and would be no addition to his few acres here in Killawaddy. Why couldn't this big lazy lump of a son of his get in tow with the Atcheson girl a few fields away? She was plump and plain and no oil painting but the wisdom of age had taught him that 'beauty fades but land is forever'. If their two farms were put together they would have a fine holding and he could step out with pride to Mass on a Sunday. With pretence at making polite conversation he slyly supplied Maggie Kate with visions of what the future held for her in the Higgins household:

'D'ye have a car, it's something that's badly needed about here?' he smiled.

'D'ye know it'd be great to have a strappin' woman like yerself here to do the cooking, cleaning and washing for the two of us? Ahh, sure there's loads to be done here from morning till night: milkin', baking and mending.'

On and on he went.

Afterwards Mickey Joe tried to placate Maggie's misgivings:

'Well you know Maggie he's full of silly talk but he has a heart of gold at the back of it,' he lied trying to make light of the encounter.

Maggie was having none of it. There was bound to be 'better fish in the sea' she thought to herself picturing Mickey's father holding forth from the kitchen bed while she slaved at the hearth fire cooking and cleaning. So she ended the relationship with Mickey, and he never again ventured to bring any woman under the old man's scrutinous glare.

Fleeting couplings he had had over the years, but now his lined and rugged jaws bore evidence of too many winter gales and hailstone showers. The constant struggle with time, the elements and a vexatious father were writ clearly on his face. He still had a good head of wiry, black, disobedient hair that, however he tried to control it, would not lie down flat. Having long ago lost his teeth, try as he might he could not wear the dentures that replaced them. They cut his gums, slipped down when he tried to speak, whistled when he used glue to hold them fast, and were eventually consigned to the dresser where they sat alongside the mugs, bowls, eggcups, letters from America and other paraphernalia that had gathered there over the years. On occasions like this however he often carried the teeth in his pocket just in case there might be a woman there that he particularly wanted to impress.

To tell the truth he was delighted at the opportunity this trip provided to cast his bread upon the water one more, and maybe last time. He had met Sally Maguire at a fair in Grange about a year before. She lived in Collooney. Being a good few miles away from Killawaddy he'd only managed to see her a few times over the course of the year. Any chance of getting to that corner of Sligo, even if it meant putting up with the irritating

Aloysius for a while, was a godsend. He thought Sally liked him. Sure he might take his courage in his fist tonight and ask her if she'd like to be buried with his people!

The thought worried and excited him all at the same time.

The little group now looked anxiously at Barney leaning out the window of the car.

'Right then,' said he laughing, 'get in the car, ye're fit for Duffy's Circus but sure the night is young and ye wouldn't know what we might hit up agin before morning. But I'm tellin' ye right away now if ye meet a woman don't think ye're going to bring her in here, ye can do yer courting out the back of the hall or wherever ye like!'

The motley crew scrambled gratefully into the car and Barney sped off down the road to Collooney, about twenty miles away. When they arrived in the village Aloysius was first out of the car and legged it off down the road as fast as he could go.

'What's up with him! Where the hell is he going?' everyone chorused.

'I feckin'well knew this was going to happen,' Barney whined as his fare disappeared off into the distance. 'Let the rest of ye not get any ideas or the whole bloody lot of ye can walk home!'

It was a bad start but Mickey Joe wasn't going to let this deter him from his mission and:

'I'll be back in a minute,' he shouted over his shoulder as he headed up the street in the opposite direction. 'Don't worry,' he added laughing, 'I'm only going up the road a bit here to see a man about a dog.'

He didn't want the rest of them to know he was going up

to see Sally. No point in making everyone as wise as himself — especially if this wasn't going to work out. She lived in a little terraced house at the top of the town and would surely be going to the dance, he thought. But what was the harm in going over there to make certain and to make sure he was in her good books for the night. As well as that he missed her — a lot. Visions of her gay and smiling face, petite form and nut-brown hair lightened his load as he worked the fields all day long under the eye of his ill-tempered father. He thought her the nicest woman he had ever met, with just enough of a veil of mischief in her eyes to worry a man.

Her mother answered his knock on the door. No, Sally's not home, she said. Will she be going to the dance tonight, Mickey enquired, trying to conceal his disappointment? Oh I don't know, she replied curtly, she's gone out for the evening; she didn't say where she was going. Thinking her somewhat evasive Mickey Joe scanned her face anxiously for clues but the old woman's dour countenance revealed nothing. Feckin' townies were a quare lot, he thought to himself as he retraced his steps down the little path and out Sally's gate.

When he returned to his fellow travellers there was a row going on. There was no dance.

No dance!

Aloysius was only saying that to get a crowd together so he could get a lift to Collooney. No one would go otherwise. One looked at the other in disbelief and then started to get on to Barney. 'It was murdher with them!' he said later.

'There's no phuckin' dance here' Mickey Joe growled, his

temper rising sharply with this unwelcome news and yet another setback to his plans for the evening. 'Ye charged us three wob to get here an' what are we going to do now? There's no dance!'

'Mickey! Will ye shut yer mouth or else put yer teeth in! Yer a sight, ye look ridiculous and I don't know half of what yer saying!'

With sour faces and dark glances the disappointed swains mumbled and muttered among themselves till:

'Arra for Chrise' sakes will ye shut up, sure we'll get a dance somewhere' Barney barked at them.'

That humoured them a bit. They brightened up and started to look for a pub.

'Come away for a drink before we go any further,' Mickey Joe said to Pat James Mulligan, his neighbour who had come along on the promise of a great night's fun.

'I would, surely to God,' says Pat, 'I'd be delighted, but I haven't a shillin' on me. I don't even know how I'm going to get in to the dance'

'Arra, don't be shtuck", said Mickey Joe gloomily, 'I have none either — but,' and his face brightened, 'I think one of the other boyos has a noggin of poteen.'

Meanwhile Barney had made enquiries and discovered there was an F.C.A. dance in Riverstown Hall a few miles away. This further cheered them up and, good humour restored, away with them in upholstered luxury off down the road once more.

As they sped through the countryside its loveliness was lost to these men on the rut. Lit by a setting sun the little green rectangles of stone-enclosed fields, climbing like a patchwork quilt along the mountains on either side, held no beauty for them. Nor did the wild display of yellow gorse that blazed 'unprofitably gay' along the mountainside, delight their eyes! 'As persistent and fertile as sin and disease' the poet of Mucker had written of the gorse bushes. These fields, like the fields they knew so well at home, were nothing more than prisons: prisons of stone that grudgingly yielded only a bare existence. The yellow gorse, joyous herald of spring, meant to them nothing more than a sure indicator of bad land; land that could be cleaned up and put to better use as pasture to feed a few extra cattle. Now there was something that made sense on a fair day! Try bringing a load of whins to sell and see what you'd get.

The talk inside the car turned to women and prospects for the night ahead. No man worth his salt was ever going to admit that he was looking for love or a lasting relationship. No! That wasn't it at all — 'twas the other thing they were looking for: 'Why buy the cow when you get the milk for free,' they sniggered.

Women inevitably were the moral guardians who laid the tender trap that steered the male of the species to the altar.

Was Mary Ann Cassidy and her fancy man going to be at the dance Barney wondered?

'The grass widow!' Mickey Joe scoffed raising his eyebrows. 'Sure the smell of the burn is off her!'

'The smell of the burn?'

'You know what I mean, second hand goods.'

'So what about it? And in any case isn't she going out with a fella this past ten years or more? Not much chance there. Time for them to make up their minds I'd say — mind you it's not easy for them what with her mother depending on her so much and no one else to look after the old woman. It's a tough spot to be in,' Barney opined.

'Where have you been? Didn't he leave her nearly a year ago now! Went off to America with a young one he met in the Silver Slipper and left her high and dry. She's back on the market again. Sued him for breach of promise and took fifty pounds off him before he could get away.'

'Breach of promise?'

'Right! Breach of promise. Jasus! Do ye know anything! If yer going out with a woman for a long time and there's an expectation of marriage an' ye decide to change your mind and feck off she can sue you! But don't worry about it, you're never going to get that close anyway!'

That got everyone's attention. There was nothing better than a bit of bad news concerning someone else's misfortune to cheer everyone up. She was 'damaged goods' now anyway and a target for chancers. In perpetual contemplation of the snares of marriage Irish men were unforgiving where women's reputations were concerned. Notwithstanding the fact that they were prepared to pluck any maidenhead that came their way, the girl they wed must be a virgin. They sought nothing less than unspoiled beauties of which, in theory at least, there were a respectable number: vouched and unvouched, imagined and asserted.

When the company had time to digest this information on the Cassidy woman's trouble: 'She'd be a good hit for you now, Mickey Joe!' Barney needled, giving his neighbour a dig in the ribs. And she has fifty pounds in the bank, maybe more!'

'Is that so then!' said Mickey rising to the bait. 'Well I'll not be takin' another man's leavings. There's plenty more fish out there than was ever caught!'

'Is that so Mickey, I'm afraid you've caught all your fish — time is moving on and and your bait gettin' a bit limp,' Barney responded, egging him on.

To hell with them, let them laugh, Mickey thought. They were just jealous. Didn't he have a woman? Sally was the object of his heart's desire and his spirits were lifted with the very thought of her; how he would soon hold her close as they waltzed around the floor that evening.

ॐ

The motley crew pulled up in a cloud of dust in front of Riverstown dancehall. Owned and operated by the parish priest the hall was a low, grey, squat, typical country hall situated on the fringe of town. It's high windows betrayed the fact that it had once served as a schoolhouse. A porch had been added to the entrance and a booth built into the corner; from a little window there money was taken and tickets handed out, sometimes by the priest himself and sometimes by one of his pious helpers. Mostly he kept a wary eye on the dancers to ensure that passions didn't flare out of hand. His divine mission was to ensure that couples went home from his dances as pure as they came. Under his watchful gaze dancing couples kept enough space between them 'to allow the Holy Ghost to pass through'. No cheek to cheek from head to toe here!

When Barney and his friends arrived at the door there was a crush and huddle of people lined up jostling to get in. This allowed Mickey Joe and Pat James to slide furtively in amid the confusion in the hope no one would notice. Inside a pall of cigarette smoke drifted towards the ceiling under which couples sat on long 'furms' along the walls. They chatted, laughed and moved about greeting friends they hadn't seen since last week's dance. Someone was spreading Lux soap flakes on the floorboards to ease the passage of dancing couples across the pitted planks that had seen better days. In the dim light a crystal ball suspended from the ceiling spun slowly sending little spangles of light and hope with counterfeit gaiety along the floor and walls.

Trouble was brewing however: Barney shortly noticed two bouncers eying him up and:

'Christ!' he whispered out of the side of his mouth to Mickey Joe. 'We're in trouble now anyway! Look at the two bucks, and one of them bigger than the other.'

The two bouncers came over to Barney right away and:

'Ye didn't pay comin' in the door,' the biggest of them announced right away sticking out his chin and squaring up to the two Killawaddy men.

'Begod', says Barney looking up at the Riverstown hulk,' 'I don't have to pay, I have a hackney badge, an' no matter where ye go in the country, the hackney badge'll get ye in free.'

It was true that taxi drivers who brought a group to a venue were admitted without charge. This encouraged them to come again with another carload of revellers.

'What kind of a car d'ye have?'

'I have a Ford Coupe.'

'Come out an' show it to us then!

Barney knew he was on safe ground now, so he went out and pointed out his pride and joy to them. It didn't help at all! They just became more annoyed. The biggest of the two hulks was out for blood and says he to Barney with great sarcasm:

'How many of ye owns the Ford Coupe? There's another buck here claiming he owns it too. What d'ye take us for?'

'Well, I have the badge here an' what more can I tell ye? Isn't that proof enough?'

Off they went then like two oversize wasps looking for the other fellow that claimed it was his. Barney went over to the car after they left and was immediately startled by a rustling in the bushes:

'Ssss. Sssss.'

Looking around he could see nothing. Then it came again, but louder.

'**Ssst. Sssst**. Over here. In the bushes!'

'Who's that?'

'It's me, Pat James, are they gone?'

Barney was hopping mad and: 'Oh! Are they gone! *Are they gone!*' he mimicked.

'Get out to feck outa the bushes! Was it you toul' them ye owned the car? Look at ye, yer as white as a ghost! An' the trouble you put me to!'

'Never mind that now! I didn't have the money to get in. Can I get into the car? If they catch me I'll be murdhered!'

'Get in the car then, ye bloody eejit! It's the last time you're going any place with me. Ye'll stay in the house the next time!'

Barney let him into the back seat of the car, covered him up with overcoats so the headhunters wouldn't discover him and strode back into the dancehall under the suspicious gaze of the two bouncers who were now on red alert. The *Clipper Carlton Showband* was playing that song of lost love, *The Tennessee Waltz*, to a few dreamy eyed couples schmoozing their way around the floor.

Unattached bachelors on one side of the hall were eyeing up the women seated along the wall on the other side. The women chatted on and powdered their noses with seeming indifference. The place was packed.

Barney surveyed the scene. The showband phenomenon was loosening whatever last tenuous hold the clergy had on passions. Covered over with a veneer of polite conversation primal passions seethed underneath the civil facade. That explosive mixture is what concerned the men of the cloth. The ballrooms and dancehalls were about meeting, romancing and sex; a new freedom was bringing to every corner of Ireland the free lifestyle lavishly portrayed at the cinema. The price of admission to the ballroom was the ticket to a mating game, a licence that often had its fulfilment in the back of a car outside after the dance, in a hayshed, at a haycock in a country field — or even at the altar.

'How would you define dancing?' Barney, winking an impish

wink, posed to Mickey Joe who was peering around intently to see if Sally was anywhere in the hall.

'Arrah! How would you define dancing!,' Mickey Joe parroted back. 'What kind of a silly question is that!

'Well it's not silly at all, it's a question.' Barney insisted. 'Go on, answer it! What would you say is a definition of dancing?'

'Well I suppose it's an ideal excuse to get talking to a perfectly strange woman that you never met before — but I have a feeling that's not the answer you're looking for!'

'Close Mickey, close! Well I'll tell ye what it is, it's the vertical expression of a horizontal desire!'

'Ah Jasus, Barney, spare yer smart chat for the women!'

Matrimony is what Mickey Joe had in mind if he could pluck up the nerve, not some tumble in the hay. Sally wasn't that kind of woman.

It was holiday time Mickey observed as he looked around.

'Barney! Would ye look at the heads on the quare fellas in the blue suits and the wide ties home from England.'

Competition, Barney thought right away. And there they were! Self confident. Assured. Hands in pockets, rattling the half crowns. When a half crown was money.

'Showin' off,' he spat. 'Would ye listen to them an' the accent, an' them not a wet week away from a boghole!'

The country lads were there too: Bikes stashed in a shed, or out the back of the hall. Don't forget to take the bicycle clips out of the trouser leg! That put everyone on a level footing. Sure you might have a car outside! Or you could pretend. A certain pull. Brilliantined hair and fag hanging nonchalantly from lower lip: who'd know; play the game. The man that forgot and left the clips in was marked out right away, a culchie, a gomshite, a pariah.

For many, more used to talking to cows in their daily routine than the opposite sex, a trip to the pub was essential preparation. Dutch courage could be had inside; theirs then the part of the cool, hard men. Women didn't go to pubs. It wasn't respectable — till the 'Baby Chams' came, an acceptable drink for a lady. It took a few years of 'liberation' for them to work their way up to a pint and a beer belly. One of the lads: 'Hi guys!'

The dance was in full swing and the boys fresh in from the pub pushing their way through the throng of youths at the edge of the dance-floor. Hunched shoulders, little swagger, fag between the fingers, blow smoke in the air. Brylcream cool and arrogant. The 'whadaya looking at, fuck you' look. If there was a fight they were going to be in it. Half sneer, half smile they looked around. Superior like. Cigarette smoke drifted towards the ceiling. A cloying sweetness of nicotine mixed with hair oil.

> *'It's now or never, come hold me tight*
> *Kiss me my darling, be mine tonight*
> *Tomorrow will be too late,*
> *It's now or never my love won't wait....'*

Dom Shearer's silky voice coaxed and teased amidst the trumpets, clarinets and trombones; bow ties, white suits, another world, another planet. Paradise was here, now, and the dream was everybody's for a night of fulfilment. Come on, they beckoned, step into our magic swirling ship:

> *'When I first saw you with your smile so tender*
> *My heart was captured, my soul surrendered*
> *I'd spend a lifetime waiting for the right time*
> *Now that you're near the time is here at last...'*

Right! That's it. It's now or never. With sidelong glances the fortified, and the unfortified, eyed the gaggle of women on the other side of the hall weighing them up. A raggle taggle lot. Emigration had taken too many away to jobs, and hope, in Dublin, England or America.

Having a strategy was essential. Some kind of plan. Ask the one you really wanted, the object of your hearts' desire, or the one you think you might be sure to get — or play it safe and ask a neighbour who was sure to oblige.

More just looked on. For them it was better to live in doubt — which is much the same as hope — than to have all one's doubts and fears proven well founded.

Suddenly Mickey Joe stiffened and went pale as a ghost.

'What's the matter with you?' Barney enquired, looking in the direction of Mickey's frozen stare — and there in a dim lit corner of the hall was the realisation of every man's worst nightmare: the love of his life sitting on his rivals knee with her arms draped affectionately around his neck. Aloysius was there with Sally! He in turn had spotted his pals of the earlier evening, wasn't expecting them, and was shrinking back into his chair.

The realisation of the treachery he was witnessing gradually overwhelmed Mickey Joe's senses. It was too much to take in. His reaction was brutal and swift.

'Look at the bastard over in the corner! Now we know why he ran off, the fuckin' traitor,' he hissed at Barney, 'An' the two eyes on him like two bubbles in a pisspot! I'll tear the fuckin' head off him,' his voice rose to a shout.

Hearing the sound of his voice Sally looked across the hall, spotted Mickey Joe, let out a scream and legged it for that refuge of all women in tight spots: the ladies toilet. Tearing off his coat as he went Mickey Joe pounded across the floor scattering dancers in all directions. Grabbing his traitorous rival by the shirt he pulled him to his feet.

'What the fuck d'ye think yer doing?' he spat with hate-filled eyes.

Mustering what was left of his courage and finding no avenue of escape — at least without looking like a coward, Aloysius shook himself free and faced his accuser.

'That's none of your business. It's a f-free country!' he managed nervously.

'Oh, it's a free country is it?, I'll show you how the fuck free it is!'

The punch that smashed into Aloysius's face took him by surprise. In a spray of blood and spittle he folded like a rag doll and went sprawling to the floor.

'Take that ye bastard and if ye want more, get up! Now! Get fuckin' up!' said Mickey his face twisted with vexation as he danced around his fallen foe his fists punching the air: right, left, right, left, leftrightleft.

'What the fuck are ye doing? Leave me alone. Let me at him,' Mickey howled as his friend Barney, having followed him across the floor, struggled to pull him away.

'Never mind! That's enough now. Ye got your own back on him, he's not worth it. And anyway isn't it her fault as much as his,' Barney soothed. 'And here's the bloody bouncers looking for trouble again. Aren't we bad enough! Shut up now and be quiet.'

It was all over as quick as it started and:

'Take yer hands off me! I'm alright,' Mickey muttered savagely as he shrugged Barney off. 'You're right, feck the two of them, they're not worth it. That's me finished with them from now on anyway. And furthermore Aloysius can walk fuckin' home. He's gettin' in no car with me!'

Hearing the commotion the two bouncers like two bloodhounds on the scent were on top of the situation right away.

'Who was it that hit you?' they inquired of Aloysius helping him up off the floor. His lip was busted and blood spurting all over his nice white shirt and tie.

'Whowasit,andbyGodwe'llseethey'llnevergetintothishallagain!'

'No one,' was all the by now thoroughly demoralised Aloysius could manage to say.

'No one? Well by Christ then whoever no one is they hammered a pretty good job on you! Tell us who it was and we'll make an example of him!'

'Never mind, leave it, I'm alright. The bastard'll get his day in court, it's not over yet.'

The band members, who had stopped playing, picked up their instruments and, 'Take your partners please for a foxtrot,' they announced from the stage.

Men drifted on to the floor again. Women, some of whom had climbed up on chairs, particularly those at the epicentre who hadn't time to make it to the toilet, climbed down again. A mouse on the floor or a fight at a dance hall were the two things that were sure to send women scurrying to a height for safety.

A buzz of excited conversation filled the air again and for those hopeful of finding love or lust it was back to business and time to put courage to the test. Top the fag. Put it behind the ear for later. On your marks, get set, GO.

The massed ranks of pimpled hopefuls charged and jostled across the floor.

'C'mon Mickey Joe,' Barney urged, 'We'll chance a few of these women over here. C'mon!'

Mickey needed little coaxing and the two joined the melee charging across the floor. He was going to show Sally that he could get a woman any night of the week. He wasn't depending on her. Or if he was he wasn't going to let it show.

'Will ye dance this wan?' he addressed a young blade about half his age he had spotted earlier on.

'Oh, I couldn't, ask me sister I'm sweatin'.'

Making a face, she gave a look to the girl beside her that said 'Jesus, some of these oul' fellas'd chance anything.'

Christ! Rejection.

Think quick.

Have to save face.

The shy lads just blushed and slunk off. Defeated. *Shot down in flames* as they would laugh later. That wasn't Mickey's way. Can't let her away with this!

'Why didn't ye bring yer knittin,' he snapped back as manfully as his sinking heart would allow.

Sometimes one refusal provoked a chain reaction all along the wall.

Chin out and chance it anyway. Put a brave face on it. Ignore the beating heart and sweating palms. Move on to the next one here showing a nice piece of leg.

'Will ye dance Miss.?'

'Buzz off, you're drunk!'

'Is that so? Well, I'll be sober in the morning but you'll still be ugly!'

That's the stuff for her. Conceity bitch!

Here's a tasty little thing here in the corner. A bit sharp looking but sure ye'd never know!

Are ye dancing Miss?'

'No! I'm particular who I dance with.'

'Well I'm not, that's why I asked you,' quick as a flash.

*'A face that'd turn milk sour,'* he muttered to himself.

Fuckin' prickteasers the lot of them.

Don't give up. Keep going.

Bzzzzz... How about this flower over here then?

And surely to God there she was: no less than Mary Ann

Cassidy herself. Wilted — and smell of the burn or not, any port in a storm is better than a shipwreck. She'd be ripe for a rub of the oul' relic! On the shelf and sure to be grateful just for being asked — and sure the shake of the bag could be the best of the flour.

'If I said you had a beautiful body would you hold it against me?' Mickey Joe offered, slick as a whistle.

Waiting for Mr. Goodbar; Mary Ann thinks quick. Will she take second offer, second choice, second best, even third?

Maybe. Maybe not. She weighs her chances. Lose face. Will I get another offer?

She'd seen the Mickey Joes of the ballrooms and dancehalls before, growing year by year into confirmed bachelorhood. Wedded to the land and oppressed by older parents. They didn't know it yet, but she could see it plain: they would never marry. The cry of a baby, the laughter of little children would never be heard around their hearthstone.

> *'...lost in the passion that never needs a wife,*
> *the pricks that pricked for them*
> *were the pointed pins of harrows...'* [11]

She thought of the man she loved and whom she believed loved her. What a fool she was. Far away in America he was now and the tears stung her eyes at the thought.

Why? Why? Why?

Why was she back here in this den of false hopes and shattered illusions to be pawed over by chancers? Here in this hall where

---

[11] *The Great Hunger*, Patrick Kavanagh

she and David had held each other, where she melted in his arms on that night long ago when he whispered in her ear, on that very dance floor, that he loved her.

'Are ye with me S-sally, I mean Mary Ann?' Mickey Joe's voice cut sharply into her musings.

There was no going back; no point in wallowing in misery:

'Laugh and the world laughs with you, weep and you weep alone'.

She looked around. Sure men were all over the place. Like a shoal of piranhas.

She couldn't miss.

'Sorry, I'm ast', she said firmly looking Mickey straight in the eye.

Having suffered the sting of rejection many times in his life Mickey Joe had another one in his arsenal. To be turned down by Mary Ann Cassidy, who in his exalted opinion wasn't exactly the pick of the crop, was more than he could bear. Looking her up and down he mustered his courage and: 'Why don't ye go home and shave!' he snarled. 'It's a long road there's no turn in.'

'Aye, and a short one there's not cowshit on!' she shot back, her gloom turning to irritation.

Christ, the smell of drink off him — and stale sweat!

∾

Is this all there was ever going to be? Was she never going to have for her own a man that appreciated a good woman? A woman who wanted nothing more in her life than a home, a house and a mate to love her for the rest of her days — and maybe, if God willed it, children.

She could see now this is where it would end. She would never experience that which sustains even the greatest wretch: the hope of being sincerely loved; to love and be loved — even if only once in their life.

> *'Spring is sprung,*
> *The grass is riz,*
> *She wonders where*
> *The good men is.'*

❧